Beekman's Big Deal

Michael de Guzman
AR B.L.: 4.1
Points: 5.0

MG

# By Michael de Guzman

Melonhead

Beekman's Big Deal

# Beekman's Big Deal

Michael de Guzman

# Beekman's Big Deal

FARRAR STRAUS GIROUX

NEW YORK

www.fsgkidsbooks.com

Library of Congress Cataloging-in-Publication Data
de Guzman, Michael.
Beekman's big deal / Michael de Guzman.— 1st ed.
    p.   cm.
Summary: Tired of the frequent moves that he and his father must make,
twelve-year-old Beekman begins to make connections with neighbors and
classmates after settling in a small, unusual New York City neighborhood.
    ISBN 0-374-30672-9
    [1. Fathers and sons—Fiction.   2. Moving, Household—Fiction.   3. Schools—
Fiction.   4. Self-realization—Fiction.]   I. Title.

PZ7.D3655Be 2004
[Fic]—dc22

2003060773

*In memory of Big Paul, the best father a boy ever had . . .*

# Beekman's Big Deal

# Prologue

Beekman O'Day, who was five years old, looked across the table at his father like he hadn't heard a word.

"Drink your milk," Leo said for the third time.

"When will my voice change?" Beekman responded. He was always asking his father that question. His voice had always been raspy, like his throat was lined with medium-grain sandpaper. When he became especially excited, his voice cracked and he croaked like a frog. They were having breakfast at a coffee shop on Madison Avenue.

"Your voice will change one of these days," Leo said as he took a felt-tip pen from his pocket and drew a line on Beekman's glass of milk. "One of these days your voice will be smooth as silk."

"It will never change," Beekman said.

"You'll sound different when you're older," Leo assured his son. "And milk will help. Just drink it down to the line."

"I don't like milk," Beekman said.

"You don't have to like it," Leo said. "All you have to do is drink it."

"Why?"

"Because it's good for you, that's why," Leo said. "It's necessary for your continued health and well-being. Your continued health and well-being is my job."

"But it tastes funny," Beekman said.

"It tastes like milk," Leo said. "Just down to the line."

"Then can I have a roll with butter and grape jelly?" Beekman asked.

"We'll see," Leo said.

Beekman and Leo had been having breakfast at this coffee shop every Monday through Friday since they'd moved into the apartment on Seventy-fourth Street. On every one of those mornings Leo had drawn lines on Beekman's glass of milk and had induced and cajoled him to drink the contents. Once a week, on Friday, if his son had consumed enough milk, he let him have his reward of a roll with butter and grape jelly.

The rest of the time he made him eat cereal, which Beekman wasn't crazy about either.

"Will I ever get any bigger?" Beekman asked. It was another favorite question.

"Drinking milk will make you bigger," Leo said. "It builds strong bones."

That was another thing Beekman O'Day knew about himself. He was small. Very small. Short and thin and wiry. The smallest kid by far at Mrs. Binkman's kindergarten. He lifted his glass and made a face and drank the milk down to the line, then made another face.

"It didn't make me any bigger," Beekman said.

"Give it time," Leo said, drawing another line an inch below the first one.

"Tell me about when I was born."

"You were born," Leo said. "It's something that happens every day. Millions of people are born." Despite his smile, Leo's well-chiseled face appeared troubled.

"Was I good-looking when I was born?"

"The best-looking baby the world has ever seen," Leo said. "Now drink your milk and eat your cereal."

"But I want to know about when I was born."

"There's nothing to know," Leo said. "We don't have time for all this conversation. We're running late."

Beekman could tell that his father was getting upset. He could hear it in his voice and see it in his expression. Leo always got upset when Beekman asked him too many questions about being born. "But I want to know," Beekman persisted. "Did I cry a lot?"

"All babies cry a lot," Leo said. "Finish your breakfast."

Beekman lifted his glass and made a face and drank his milk down to the next line, then made another face.

Ten minutes later they were standing on the sidewalk in front of Mrs. Binkman's kindergarten. Beekman's hands were planted firmly on his hips. His chin was thrust out defiantly. "I'm not going," he said.

"You have to go," Leo said. "You have school and I have work. That's the deal."

"I don't like that deal," Beekman said.

"It's the deal we have," Leo said. "You know you like it once you're there."

"I don't like it," Beekman said. He dropped to his knees and banged his forehead against the pavement. "I'm not going!" he yelled.

Leo snatched Beekman up off the ground, checked his head for damage—none was done—wiped away the smudge of sidewalk grit, and carried him inside.

"I don't like school," Beekman protested, wriggling in his father's arms. "I hate it."

6

# 1

## Up and at 'Em

The telephone rang. Beekman hated the telephone. It interrupted things. Like sleep. It rang again. He could hear his father singing opera in the shower. Leo always sang opera in the shower, even though he didn't know the words to a single one. It rang again. Answering the telephone meant getting out of bed. Beekman hated getting out of bed before he was ready. It rang again. Reluctantly, he hauled his bony little twelve-year-old body from beneath the sheets and padded across the wilted green carpet to the desk and picked up the receiver.

"Good morning, Rudy," Beekman said in his raspy voice.

"Good morning to you, Beekman," Rudy said. "Up and at 'em."

"I am up and at 'em, Rudy," Beekman said. "I couldn't be talking to you if I wasn't up and at 'em."

"That's the spirit," Rudy said. Rudy worked the night desk at the Chester Hotel. His last duty before going home was to make sure that Beekman was out of bed. Leo had arranged it. In case he overslept himself. Beekman and Leo lived in suite 1501, which was two rooms plus kitchenette, complete with peeling paint and fading wallpaper. Leo slept in the bedroom. Beekman slept in the sitting room, which was sometimes Leo's office. He slept on a Murphy bed, which was hidden behind a door and pulled down from the wall. Sometimes Beekman wondered what it would be like to be folded up into the wall with it.

"I'm awake, Rudy," Beekman said. "I promise I won't go back to bed. You can go home now."

"Then home I'll go," Rudy said. "It's going to be seventy-eight degrees today and not a drop of rain in the sky. Good luck with the interview."

"Thank you, Rudy," Beekman said. He hung up. He liked Rudy, whom he hardly ever saw because their schedules were so different. Rudy was eighty years old. Beekman yawned and stretched and made his way to the window and looked down at Ninth Avenue. He liked how small everything was down there; people the size of pinky fingers, buses that looked like toys. He heard his father singing "Seventy-six Trombones," which meant it was his turn.

"Hi ya, Pop," Beekman said as he entered the steam-filled bathroom with its cracked tile floor and old-fashioned toilet, whose water tank was braced precariously above it close to the ceiling. He thought the tank's long pull chain should have a whistle attached to it. Some big old whomper of a whistle that sounded like a train coming to a crossing, or maybe a ship's foghorn. Every toilet in the city should have one. Millions of horns and whistles going off all day. They'd hear it on the planet Pluto.

"Hello, my one and only son," Leo said, wiping at the mirror so he could see his face to shave. Leo had a ready smile and straight white teeth and a full head of coal-black hair. "Good night's sleep?"

"Good until Rudy called," Beekman said.

"How is Rudy this morning?"

"On his way home."

"To the enchanted land of Brooklyn."

Beekman stepped out of his underwear and turned on the shower. Leo ran the razor down his right cheek. "Big day today," he said.

"What's big about it?" Beekman said, stepping under the water.

"Your interview is what's big about it," Leo said. "On top of which, there is no such thing as a small day. They're all big."

Beekman didn't think that an interview with yet another new school qualified as a big day. Especially when the fall term had already started. Four days ago. But he kept this to himself. He'd been to too many schools to make an issue of it.

"Think big, live big," Leo said.

"Think small, live small," Beekman said.

"Now you're talking," Leo said. He started singing "Over the Rainbow."

Beekman washed his hair, which was brown and grew in several directions at once and fell forward over his forehead, no matter how much effort he put into training it. He soaped his body. There wasn't an ounce of fat on him. His rib cage looked like a section of bumpy road. He thought that a truly big day would be one in which absolutely nothing happened.

While Leo ironed their shirts, Beekman made his bed and pushed it up into its alcove and closed the door. He slid the coffee table back into position. It was where they ate breakfast.

"Groats grip the road," Leo said, spooning out two

bowls of it from the pot on the three-burner stove. He'd done somebody a favor and ended up with a hundred-pound bag of the stuff by way of thanks. There were a lot of groats left.

"Groats are for horses," Beekman said. He hated groats.

"Groats are oats," Leo said. "Like oatmeal and so on. Groats are good for you."

Beekman whinnied. He sounded like a horse with a frog in its throat.

Leo laughed. It was hard to stay mad at Leo. He had a way of looking at you that made it difficult to remember why you were angry. He had a way of making you want to make him happy.

"Think how fast you'll be able to run if you eat groats," Leo said. He poured milk on his and passed the container to Beekman. He sprinkled brown sugar on top.

"Maybe if I eat enough groats," Beekman said, "I'll turn into a horse." He poured the absolute minimum amount of milk required over his groats, then added two heaping tablespoons of brown sugar. He wished he had some chocolate syrup and ice cream to top it off.

Beekman poured them each a glass of orange juice. Leo poured himself a cup of coffee. Beekman measured out half a glass of milk, then added two table-spoons of coffee. They pulled chairs to the table. Leo passed Beekman the *Daily News* and opened *The New York Times*.

"How'd you find this school?" Beekman asked after scanning the front page of the paper for the various scandals and sensational crimes that had occurred in the past twenty-four hours.

"The result of my never-ending search for a better life," Leo said. "Chance Academy is a fully accredited institution with an outstanding academic program. You're being interviewed this morning by none other than Headmaster McCann himself."

"What if I don't get in?" Beekman asked. "School has already started. Maybe they don't have room."

"They have room for one smart boy," Leo said.

"That leaves me out," Beekman said.

"You'll get in," Leo said. "You always do."

"I don't get to stay very long."

"You can't complain about your education," Leo said, putting down the newspaper. "You're the smartest kid I know. You're smarter than ninety-nine percent of the people I do business with. You're way ahead of the game."

Beekman thought about all the schools he'd been to since Mrs. Binkman's kindergarten. He'd been to

St. David's, Trinity, McBurney, Ethical Culture, St. Ignatius, Horace Mann, Brandeis Prep, and Winkler's School for the Performing Arts. He could no longer remember the exact order in which he'd attended them. He swallowed a spoonful of groats and, despite the brown sugar and milk, felt like he was grazing in a field.

"Why is it called Chance Academy?" Beekman asked when he managed to swallow.

"It's named for its founder, Ulysses S. Chance," Leo said. "Mr. Chance hit it big and wanted to give something back, so he started this school."

"For who?"

"For boys who are smarter than they think they are."

"No girls?"

"No girls."

"Why'd they agree to interview me when school's already started?"

"I convinced Headmaster McCann that you were a bright prospect. Not to be overlooked. Worth the trouble. I described you and he agreed."

"I got all C's last year," Beekman said. "Technically I didn't even finish. I had to leave ten days early."

"I told you I was sorry about that. You can go ten days extra this year if it makes you happy."

"Why are you so sure they'll take me?"

"Name one school that hasn't taken you," Leo said. "Nobody can resist an O'Day. Stop worrying so much and eat your groats."

"Somebody owed you something, didn't they?"

"Somebody who knows somebody who is an illustrious graduate of Chance Academy put in a word. All I got you was the interview. The rest is up to you. Will Beekman O'Day take advantage of the situation? Will Beekman O'Day become an illustrious graduate of Chance Academy himself? Stay tuned."

An unlikely prospect, Beekman thought, given that the probability of his completing even one full year at Chance Academy was practically nil. And that wasn't just because he was something less than an ideal student and often in trouble because his behavior left something to be desired. Many times it was because Leo ran out of money and couldn't pay the bill.

"Why don't you just send me to public school?" Beekman asked his father as they stood side by side in front of the full-length mirror in the hall. Leo was wearing his light gray suit, one of a half dozen he'd had tailored when they were flush. He wore a white shirt and a black knit necktie and dark brown English suede shoes. Beekman was decked out in dark gray flannel pants, white shirt, one of Leo's old black knit ties, blue blazer, and black lace-up shoes. This was pretty much Leo's understanding of the Chance Academy uniform.

"I went to public school," Leo said. "My son will do better."

It was what his father always said. Beekman had often pointed out that public school was free, but Leo didn't care. His mind was closed on the subject. His son was going to private school no matter what. Beekman wondered what public school would be like. At the very least the possibility of staying put would be greatly increased.

Leo tucked his silk handkerchief down into the breast pocket of his jacket, then put his hand on Beekman's shoulder. "If there's a better-looking father-and-son combo in America," he said, "I don't know where they're hiding."

Beekman studied his image in the mirror. He was short and reedy thin and his ears stuck out a little too far and he carried a serious expression, as though he had something important permanently on his mind. But even with all that, he had to admit that he didn't look half bad. His nose and eyes and mouth were all in the right place and about the right size for the rest of him. He shifted his gaze upward to take in his father's reflection and saw that Leo was smiling at him. He smiled back.

They sang a chorus of "Tea for Two" and did a little dance to go with it, then headed out. Mr. Bush, who was the assistant manager of the Chester Hotel, was waiting for them in the lobby.

"Good morning, Mr. O'Day," Mr. Bush said to Leo. "I wonder if I might have a word with you." He didn't even look at Beekman.

"Of course, Mr. Bush," Leo said. "Would three o'clock this afternoon be convenient?" Leo liked to set the time and place of meetings.

"I was hoping we could do it now," Mr. Bush said.

Beekman thought that Mr. Bush always looked like he'd just got done sucking on a lemon.

"Nothing would give me greater pleasure," Leo said, "but I have an important meeting for which I am already late. Three o'clock would be excellent, but I can also do it at five. Why don't we do it at five? For a drink. That way the problems of the day will be behind us and we can relax. Meet me at the Plaza at five. The bar at the Oak Room." Leo moved to the large glass doors that led to the street. Beekman stayed one step ahead of him.

"Three o'clock will be fine," Mr. Bush said, smiling like he had gas. "My office."

"In the lobby," Leo said, as Wilbur, resplendent in his faded brown uniform with its tarnished gold piping, pulled one of the doors open.

"Good morning," Wilbur said in a voice that sounded like it came out of his nose.

"Good morning, Wilbur," Leo and Beekman said in unison.

"Do you need a taxi this morning?" Wilbur asked.

"No, thank you," Leo said. "I'm walking."

"No, thank you, Wilbur," Beekman said.

They stopped at the corner to survey the day. The sun was brilliant against a deep blue September sky. They inhaled the morning air.

"Why does Mr. Bush want to see you?" Beekman asked.

"Mr. Bush moves in mysterious ways," Leo said.

"Is he going to throw us out?"

Leo grinned. "We don't get thrown out," he said. "We leave."

"Are we behind with the rent?"

"Hey, who handles the finances in this outfit?" Leo said. "I'll do my job, you do yours. Besides, I'm working on a big one. A life-changer."

Deals were Leo's business. He was always making

one or setting one up or just missing out on one. But it was the life-changer he was after. The one that would set them up forever.

"What kind of deal?" Beekman asked. He was anxious for his father to succeed.

"Basically it involves an amusement park in California and a fleet of old ships in Turkey and some people in Singapore who want to buy them. I'm one meeting and five phone calls away from putting it together."

"Knock 'em dead, Pop," Beekman said.

"You too, son of mine," Leo said. "Show them at that school what an O'Day is made of."

Beekman watched his father walk off as though he didn't have a care in the world. Leo moved gracefully. He was relaxed. At peace with his surroundings. He exuded confidence. Nothing flustered Leo. Beekman wanted to be that way. He pulled his Mets cap down over his eyes and headed uptown. He walked as leisurely as his father, doing his best to emulate him. So what if he was late for his interview?

# 2

# The Interview

Beekman made his unhurried way up Columbus Avenue to Eighty-eighth Street, then headed toward Amsterdam Avenue until he reached his destination. The four-story stone mansion that had once been the home of Ulysses S. Chance stood wedged between two modern apartment buildings like the overstuffed contents of a huge white-bread sandwich. Now it was Chance Academy, founded and endowed in 1901 by this minor robber baron whose fortune was made manufacturing railroad track. It was all rooftop turrets and gargoyles and dormers and high arched windows and spiked iron fences and carved double doors of dark brown wood. Beekman suspected that he might find Gomez and Morticia and Lurch and the rest of the Addams family waiting for him inside.

It was just Lurch. In the person of Headmaster McCann. Who was the largest person Beekman had ever seen. It hurt his neck to look up at the six-foot-seven-inch-tall frowning man whose facial features and girth were directly proportional to his height.

"You're enormous," Beekman said.

"And you're late, Mr. O'Day," Headmaster McCann said, tucking his watch back into his vest pocket. His voice was as large as the rest of him.

"But—" Beekman started to say.

"There are no *but*s at Chance Academy," Headmaster McCann said, cutting him off.

"There was a lot of traffic," Beekman said, undeterred. "There were a lot of people on the street."

"Take the subway," Headmaster McCann said.

"Oh, I couldn't take the subway," Beekman responded. "It's underground. I don't like traveling underground."

"Tardiness is not on the program at Chance Academy, Mr. O'Day. You can walk. You can run. You can fly. How you transport yourself is of no concern to me. When you get here is. I'm Headmaster McCann. I like to greet prospective students personally." Headmaster

McCann strode off across the polished marble floor of the building's grand entrance.

"I needed time to think about what I was going to say this morning," Beekman said, trying to keep up. "I'm a little nervous about the interview." He followed the headmaster through the outer office, past the school secretary.

"Miss Haymaker, this is Mr. O'Day," Headmaster McCann announced as he sped by. "He may or may not be our new student."

"It's good to meet you," Beekman said to Miss Haymaker, extending his hand and pumping hers briskly.

"You're late," Miss Haymaker said.

"Sometimes things happen," Beekman said.

"And sometimes they don't," Miss Haymaker said.

"Come along," Headmaster McCann said.

Beekman entered the inner office, the inner sanctum, the mighty McCann's lair. It was book-lined and thickly carpeted and the walls were painted a dark forest green. A large globe stood on its stand in one corner. A portrait of the portly Ulysses S. Chance filled the space above the fireplace.

"You sit there and I'll sit here and we'll size each other up," the mighty McCann said.

Beekman settled in at one end of the long couch

and the mighty McCann lowered himself slowly onto the other and they eyed each other.

"You have a good-looking school here," Beekman said finally, thinking to break the ice on a positive note.

"You've been to a lot of schools," the mighty McCann said.

"There are reasons for that," Beekman said in a practiced way. He prepared himself to recite them.

"No need to explain," the mighty McCann said. "Your father covered all that when we spoke. Charming man, your father. Solid. Old school. Who was the second president of the United States?"

"John Adams," Beekman said. It wasn't that he hadn't paid attention in all the schools he'd attended. He'd learned a little something.

"We don't have computers at Chance. We don't offer electives. We don't play sports with other schools. There are no gut courses. We have a prescribed program that teaches our students to read, to think, to solve problems, and to express themselves. All our students take the same course of study. If you manage to graduate from Chance, you'll possess the tools to educate yourself for the rest of your life. Where is Lake Titicaca?"

"South America."

"Where in South America?"

"Peru. Ecuador. Chile. Somewhere in there." He remembered studying the lake. Who could forget its name once heard? "The best Panama hats are made in Ecuador." Maybe he'd get some extra credit for throwing that in.

"Why should we be interested in Lake Titicaca?"

"It's the highest lake in the world."

"What's the square root of one hundred forty-four?"

"I don't know."

"Take a guess."

"I couldn't."

"What is a square root?"

"I don't remember."

"Look at it another way," the mighty McCann said. "What number times itself equals one hundred forty-four?"

"That's a tough one," Beekman said. He stunk at math. He hated math.

"What's twelve times twelve?"

Beekman calculated quickly: Ten times twelve was one hundred twenty. Easy. Then two times twelve was twenty-four, which, added to one hundred twenty, came to one hundred forty-four. "It's one hundred forty-four," he said. "So the square root of one hundred forty-four is twelve."

"The chapel, my office, Miss Haymaker, and the library are on the main floor," the mighty McCann said. "Chapel begins precisely at nine. We sing a song to kindle the spirit, read something to stimulate the mind, and make announcements. That takes fifteen minutes. Five minutes later the first class of the day begins. We are precise at Chance, Mr. O'Day. Things are as they were meant to be. Who was Stephen Crane?"

"A writer."

"Who wrote what?"

"*The Red Badge of Courage*."

"Which you've read."

"It takes place during the Civil War. It's about a boy's first experience in battle."

"The upper school," the mighty McCann said, "grades ten, eleven, and twelve, or forms four, five, and six as we refer to them here, meets on the third floor. The gym and lunchroom are on the fourth floor. There's a playing field in back. Intramural sports are mandatory. What's your personal philosophy of life?"

"To stay in one place as long as I can," Beekman said.

"The lower school, grades seven, eight, and nine, or forms one, two, and three, meets on the second floor.

There are twenty young men in each form. I know everything that goes on here. The classical education offered by Chance remains unchanged since the death of our founder. The terms of his endowment assure its future. Neatness in appearance and schoolwork matters. Spell *college*."

"*C-o-l-l-e-g-e*."

"Come with me." The mighty McCann charged out of his office. Once again Beekman had to pass the formidable Miss Haymaker. "He didn't eat you," Miss Haymaker said. "That's a good sign."

In the library, the mighty McCann pulled textbooks from shelves. "Latin," he said. "Mathematics. Science. History. Government studies. Do you prefer Spanish or French?"

"Spanish," Beekman said. "Does this mean I'm accepted?" He thought it would be nice to hear the words. Some small bit of ceremony. A moment's recognition.

"We're out of philosophy books right now," the mighty McCann said. "I'll order one. It includes the study of comparative religions. A boy withdrew two days ago for health reasons. Your father's timing was fortuitous." He stacked the books in Beekman's arms. "In addition to all this, you'll take physical education.

A strong mind requires a strong body to transport it." He tucked a piece of paper under Beekman's chin. "Your class schedule. It changes every day."

Weighed down like a pack mule, Beekman ran to keep up as the mighty McCann took his giant steps across the marble floor to the grand sweeping marble staircase. Up they went, directly to a closed classroom door on the second floor. The mighty McCann flung it open.

"Mr. Gno," the mighty McCann bellowed at the startled teacher, "this is Mr. Beekman O'Day." He put a hand on Beekman's back and pushed him into the room.

"Don't let me down," the mighty McCann said to Beekman.

# 3

## Promises to Keep

Chance Academy disgorged its contents promptly at three-thirty. One hundred twenty young men hit the pavement on the run, yelling at one another, calling one another names, making plans, roughhousing, or, in a few cases, just walking off quietly. Beekman's first day at Chance was the last of the week for the other one hundred and nineteen. It was Friday.

Beekman made his way quickly to Columbus Avenue, his eyes to the ground, avoiding contact with his dispersing classmates, especially one Marcus Peavy, who'd spent a large part of the day trying to befriend him. He didn't want to be friends with Marcus Peavy. Or anybody else. He headed down Columbus, then made his way toward Central Park and the zoo. He hated the zoo, but he loved the animals it imprisoned.

He bought a hot dog with an extra thick slathering of mustard. He found an unoccupied bench and sat. The zoo was filled with little kids and their mothers, filled with shrieks of laughter and the demand for balloons and ice cream. Beekman had come here with Leo when he was a little kid. First it was the children's zoo with the petting animals. Then came the real one, with the monkeys and elephants and snakes. When he was older, he'd started coming on his own. He'd started making his way around Manhattan from wherever they were living to wherever he was going to school and back, and to the deli and museums and other places he felt like going to when he was ten. Double digits made him old enough and wise enough to negotiate the city's streets. He knew the bus routes, but mostly he walked.

He finished his hot dog and went to visit the polar bears and to reflect on his first day at Chance. Mr. Gno, whose hair looked like his finger was permanently stuck in an electrical socket, had taught math like an army drill instructor. Mr. Nussbaum had mumbled his way through a story in Latin, not a word of which Beekman recognized. Señor Gomez, his Spanish teacher, spoke so fast that it all came out like one enormously long, unintelligible word. His English teacher, Mr. Fiddler, had looked around the classroom the whole period like he couldn't remember where he was. Mr. Maroni had read his American history lecture from index cards that were so old they looked like they'd dissolve in his hands. Mr. Jack had taught government studies and physical education as though they were pretty much the same thing. He was short and thin and wore huge round glasses with thick lenses and a business suit at all times. Mr. Keen, the science teacher, had seemed perpetually on the verge of tears, as though some tragedy that only he could see was about to befall them all. Philosophy didn't meet on Friday, so Dr. Tarter remained a mystery.

As for Headmaster McCann, the mighty McCann, Beekman was on the one hand grateful that the colossus had taken him in, and on the other dismayed that he'd ended up at a school that was so peculiar and demanding. He concluded that it would be best to avoid the mighty McCann whenever possible. He'd figure out how to deal with the rest of them. He'd do what he had to do and no more. Just as he'd done at all his other schools. He wouldn't let himself care about any of it so that when he had to leave and go someplace else, it wouldn't matter. He paid his respects to the penguins and wandered home to the Chester Hotel.

"I take it they accepted you," Leo said as Beekman dropped his books on the coffee table with a loud thump at ten minutes after five. Leo was at the desk writing on a yellow legal pad.

"I'm in," Beekman said. "Are we out? Is that what Mr. Bush wanted?"

"We're never out, son of mine," Leo said. "And good for you. I knew you'd make it."

Beekman stripped off his blazer and necktie. "What about Mr. Bush?" he asked. He poured himself a glass of apple juice.

"There's less to him than meets the eye, I'll tell you that," Leo said, tearing a sheet from the yellow pad and adding it to the pile of completed pages. "We'll celebrate tonight."

"Celebrate what?"

"You. Me. Us. We'll do it right. You'll tell me about your day and I'll tell you about mine. We'll tell each other amazing things."

"What about Mr. Bush?"

"Mr. Bush can wait his turn," Leo said.

Chinese food was Beekman's favorite, and Mr. Chin's was his favorite restaurant. It was all black granite and smoked glass inside and it was very popular with the West Side crowd. Leo had helped Mr. Chin in some way a long time ago. Mr. Chin couldn't do enough for Leo and his son. There was never a bill.

"You're getting bigger, Beekman," Mr. Chin said as he led them to the quiet corner where he always kept a small table available in case somebody important walked in. He always said that Beekman was getting bigger, even when he wasn't.

"I'm the same size as last time," Beekman said.

"You look bigger," Mr. Chin said, undeterred. He yelled at a passing waiter to bring water and tea and a beer for Leo and a ginger ale for Beekman and a green onion pancake. He told the waiter to run.

When the waiter brought all that, Beekman and Leo ordered shrimp pot stickers, chicken in black bean sauce, and a dish of Mr. Chin's famous handmade noodles.

"So tell me about Chance Academy," Leo said when they were alone. "Obviously the interview went well."

"He asked me a bunch of questions, I gave him a bunch of answers," Beekman said. "It seemed like he was going to take me no matter what I said."

"Not true," Leo said.

"Well, it couldn't be much of a school if they took me at the last minute."

"You underestimate yourself," Leo said.

"I don't like school," Beekman said.

"Maybe this is the year you change your mind," Leo said. "What have they got you studying?"

Beekman told him. He left out his description of the teachers and his concerns about Latin and math. He told Leo that there were no computers and no sports teams and that he didn't care about either of them.

"So it's going to be all right," Leo said.

"It's going to be all right," Beekman said. He wanted it to be all right. He hoped it would be all right. He had no faith in the idea.

"Things work out, my one and only son," Leo said. "Not always the way you think they will, but they work out."

"Mr. Bush said we had to leave, didn't he?"

"A better situation has presented itself," Leo said.

"I don't want a better situation," Beekman said.

"We have to keep moving forward," Leo said. "Forward is the direction of life."

"I don't want to keep moving forward," Beekman said. "I'm tired of moving."

The Chester Hotel wasn't the best place they'd ever lived in. It wasn't the worst. But it was the fourteenth place they'd lived in since Beekman's birth. It had the distinct advantage of being where they were at the moment.

"We have a three-month trial on a mews house," Leo said.

"What's a mews house?" Beekman asked. "It sounds like a place for cats."

"That's a good one," Leo said. "A mews is a private alley that's lined with small attached houses. It's three months for practically nothing. Somebody moved out unexpectedly. The deal is too good to pass up."

"We're going to live in our own house?" Beekman asked. They'd lived in rooms, apartments, and hotels, but never in a house.

"A very small house," Leo said.

"It will be all ours?"

"If we like it. After three months. We can buy it then if we want to stay."

"To stay in for as long as we want?"

"Positively," Leo said. "If we want it. If everything works out."

"Permanently?"

"I'm getting as tired of moving as you are," Leo said.

"Forever?"

"This could be the place," Leo said.

"You're sure about all this?" Beekman asked. He had to keep hearing it.

"I'm sure," Leo said.

"One hundred percent sure?"

"One hundred percent," Leo said.

"So, it's a deal?"

"It's a deal," Leo said. "We'll both do our best and we'll find a way to make it happen." Leo stuck out his hand.

Beekman shook it. "Okay," he said, "it's a deal."

# 4

## Moving

Beekman stood on the hydraulic tailgate of the battered old truck that his father had gotten his hands on somewhere. He pulled the lever that operated it and he was jerked upward. For the length of the ride he was on one of those construction-site elevators, those birdcages that lift you to the clouds. He could picture himself up there, walking the girders high above the city, his hard hat set at a jaunty angle, his welding visor flipped up, his torch ready to spew blue flame. He was fearless. The master of his destiny. The tailgate shuddered to a stop. He rode it back down. It clanged as it hit the street. He rode it up again. This time he was a fighter pilot heading to the flight deck of his aircraft carrier to be catapulted into the heavens.

At the top he stepped into the truck and looked around, taking visual inventory. Boxes of books and clothes, and shopping bags filled with bathroom and kitchen odds and ends, were packed tight into one corner. Lining the wall next to them were the stereo and CDs, and Leo's typewriter. The two paintings they owned came after that; one of them was of a Spanish guitar player, the other was of wild horses. His gaze came to rest on the old leather suitcase that Leo had carted with them every time they'd moved. Beekman had never seen the suitcase opened. One day soon he'd look inside. When he was ready.

He sat on the floor and leaned against the side and looked out the back of the truck. He saw a snap of lightning and a moment later heard a roll of thunder. It began to rain. The drops were the size of dimes. It was Saturday, the morning after their dinner at Mr. Chin's. Beekman was upset. Leo had yelled at him for coming back into the hotel when he'd been told to stay in the truck. Leo's words still stung.

"Can't you follow a simple direction?"

"I want to help."

"You can help by staying in the truck."

"It's boring in the truck."

"Tough noogies. Get back there. Pronto."

"All right. I'm going. I'm sorry."

"Sorry won't cut it if somebody steals our stuff."

Beekman was also a little depressed. They were leaving what he knew and heading into uncharted territory. It always depressed him when he moved from one place to another. There was always something or somebody to be missed. Rudy would never call to wake him again. Wilbur wouldn't be there to greet him in the morning. His bed wouldn't come down out of the wall. Moving meant new people. New circumstances. New routines. But this move was different. If things worked out, and Beekman had already convinced himself that they would, they'd never have to pack again. Depression gave way to excitement.

When they pulled away from the hotel, Leo was smiling. "I've got a surprise for you," he said.

"I don't like surprises," Beekman said. He liked things out in the open where he could see them. He greatly preferred to know what was going to happen next.

"You'll like this one," Leo said.

"Tell me what it is."

"We're stopping somewhere on the way to Nutting

Court," Leo said. "That's all I'm telling you." Nutting Court was the name of the mews where their new house was.

Leo drove them downtown, then over toward the Hudson River. To a low, flat building that looked like it had been long abandoned. Leo honked the truck's horn; three long, three short. The metal door in front of them was sucked up out of the way and they drove inside, where they were met by a young man with a shaved head named Hector.

"Everything's ready, Mr. O'Day," Hector said. He looked like he was made out of rock. His arms were as big around as Beekman's body. The door closed behind them.

"Come on," Leo said.

Beekman jumped down from the truck and followed his father and Hector into an airplane hangar of a room that was filled from one end to the other with furniture. All kinds of furniture. Row after row of furniture.

"Pick out a bed and a desk and a chair and a bookcase for your room," Leo said.

"Whatever I want?" Beekman couldn't believe it.

"Don't go crazy," Leo said. "It's a small room. Keep it simple."

"Who does all this belong to?" Beekman asked.

"I made a deal," Leo said. "I got my hands on some airline tickets and traded them. It's okay, my son. Have a blast."

Beekman hardly knew where to begin. He went down one aisle and up another, choosing this and that, then just as quickly changing his mind when he saw something he liked better. He could tell that everything had been used before, but he didn't care. It had his name on it now.

An hour later, the truck was making its way slowly through the rain to the East Side. The wiper blades slapped lazily back and forth; *rap-rup, rap-rup*. Beekman sat between his father and Hector.

"Here's something you might not know," Beekman said. "When ducks sleep, the last duck in line sleeps with one eye open so it can see if anything is trying to sneak up on them. That's the guard duck."

"That's amazing," Hector said.

Leo glanced at his son. "You make that up?"

"Who knows?" Beekman answered. Sometimes he couldn't remember where his information came from. Sometimes it seemed like it was just there, like water waiting to be released from the tap. Anyway, he liked the idea of being able to sleep with one eye open.

"Here's another one," Beekman said. "When a pack of wolves travels through the snow, they walk single file so they can step in the tracks made by the leader. That way they don't have to work so hard and get worn out. When the lead wolf gets tired, it goes to the back of the line and the next wolf takes over."

"That's amazing," Hector said.

"You're a barrel of information today," Leo said.

"Sometimes I surprise myself," Beekman said.

"You know what they say," Leo said, bringing the truck to a creaky stop at a traffic light.

"What do they say?" asked Beekman, even though he knew the answer.

"You can pick your nose and you can pick your friends, but you can't pick your friend's nose."

"That's an old one," Beekman said, laughing.

"The good ones never get old," Leo said, putting the truck in gear. They lurched forward.

"How about some music?" Hector said. He turned on the radio.

"It's broken," Leo said. "You can't be fussy when the truck is free."

"I'll sing," Beekman offered. To the tune of "Stars and Stripes Forever," he belted out in his raspy voice: "Be kind to your web-footed friends, for a duck may be somebody's father. You may think that this is the end, and it is." Then, making goggles by turning his hands upside down and making circles with his fingers, he swung right into: "Up in the air, junior bird-man, up in the air upside down . . ."

"You know what the trouble with the world today is?" Leo asked when his son was finished.

"Too many comedians," Beekman said.

"You've got that right," Leo said. He swung the truck onto Thirty-eighth Street and headed toward the East River.

"Almost there," Leo said.

# 5

## A Room of His Own

"Hey, you!"

The heavy rain had given way to a fine, soft mist.
The sun had turned the day hazy bright. An electric
rainbow arced through the sky to the east, somewhere
over Long Island.

"Hey, you, elephant ears!"

Beekman ignored the voice, even though he knew it
was directed at him. He paid no attention to the rainbow. He didn't feel the mist brushing his face. He was
standing on the hydraulic tailgate of the truck staring
transfixed at the cobblestone alley and the eight small
two-story attached houses that comprised Nutting
Court. He loved it. He loved the house that was his,

the first one on the right. The one into which his father and Hector were presently moving their newly acquired furniture.

"What? You deaf or something? I'm talking to you, snot-head!" The driver who was yelling at Beekman was bald and candy-apple red in the face with rage. "Hey, moron boy, where's the entrance to the Midtown Tunnel?"

"Who you calling moron, cue ball?" a new voice hollered. Beekman couldn't see who the voice belonged to. "You got a problem, try me," the voice yelled. It didn't sound like somebody Beekman would want to mess with.

"Fruitcake!" the driver screamed as he drove away with a squeal of his tires.

"Chrome-dome imbecile," the voice yelled back. A moment later a large, thick man appeared from the sidewalk side of the truck. He was in his fifties. He carried a brightly colored umbrella. He was wearing a floral print dress that ended at his ankles.

"You can't let a creep like that bother you," the man said, looking up at Beekman.

"He didn't bother me," Beekman said. "But thank you for the help."

"Not worth the aggravation," the man said.

"Life's too short," Beekman said.

"I'm Moxie LaMoca," the man said. "I used to be a boxer. Light heavyweight. Won nineteen. Lost nineteen. When I started seeing two of everything I quit. You're the new people."

"I'm Beekman O'Day," Beekman said. He lowered the tailgate and stepped off and shook Moxie LaMoca's big, callused ham of a hand.

"A pleasure to make your acquaintance, Beekman O'Day," Moxie LaMoca said. "You and your father are moving into number eight. I'm in number one. Right across from you. Fernanda Bloom, she's in number two. Edna and Larry Biggs are in three. Sergio West is in four. Madam de Campo is in five. Loomis Garcia is in six. Minnie and Manfried Mumm are in seven. Most of us have been here forever. You'll get to know everybody. Everybody will get to know you. We keep an eye on each other. That's how it is at Nutting Court."

Beekman studied the mews. There were three attached houses on each side of the cobblestone alley and two in the back that faced the street. There were flowers everywhere; in pots and window boxes and in the small planted areas in front of each house. Each door was painted a different color; brown, red, yellow, green, purple, orange, blue, and rose. The houses themselves were all creamy white with black roofs. A small brick chimney jutted into the air above each of them. At the center of the alley was a fountain that gurgled water. Behind it grew a nearly perfect Japanese maple tree.

"Why is it called Nutting Court?" Beekman asked.

"It was built by Thomas Nutting in 1889," Moxie LaMoca responded. "For his family. He had seven children. Enough said. I have to change for work."

"What kind of work do you do?" Beekman called out after him. "If you don't mind my asking."

"Not at all," Moxie LaMoca said, looking back. "Nights, I'm a singing waiter at Marciano's. Days, I'm a street performer. I do impressions. Today I'm Barbra Streisand. What do you think?" He made a slow turn.

"You look good in that dress," Beekman said.

"I made it myself," Moxie LaMoca said. He offered up a few bars of "People" in a rich tenor voice as he headed into his house.

Beekman stepped back on the tailgate and rode it to the top. If Moxie LaMoca wanted to wear a dress, that was fine with Beekman. He didn't care who lived at Nutting Court or what they did. This was going to be his home.

When the last box was unloaded and Hector had driven off in the truck, Beekman went upstairs to his room and parked himself in front of his window. His own window. In his own room. Which was approximately fourteen feet long and eight feet wide. It was at the top of the short, steep staircase that began just inside the front door. It was the only room upstairs. Not counting the storage area, which was reached through a door at the back of his closet, it was all the upstairs there was. The one small window provided him with a view of the alley and fountain and tree, and a decent stretch of sidewalk and street, and all the houses of Nutting Court except for the two right next to his. With his single bed, bedside table, desk, chair, bureau, and bookcase in place, there was just enough room for him to maneuver about. He was joyously happy with it. Downstairs was the living room and dining area, kitchen, bathroom, and Leo's bedroom. This was his.

"You doing okay up there?" It was Leo calling from the bottom of the stairs.

"I am," Beekman answered. "You doing okay down there?"

"You bet. Mind if I come up?"

"Come up," Beekman said. He heard the stairs creaking under his father's weight. It was an excellent security system. Almost as good as a one-eyed sleeping duck. He watched Leo bend to get through the doorway, which was just a shade over five feet high.

The ceiling in his room was no more than five feet six.

"Nice layout," Leo said. He couldn't stand up straight. He was two inches too tall. He tried bending at the waist. He tried bending his knees.

"You can sit on my bed if you want to," Beekman said. He'd already made it, tucking the sheets and blanket in together with hospital corners at the foot. You couldn't bounce a quarter on it, but there weren't any wrinkles either.

Beekman pulled himself up to sit on his desk.

Leo sat and rubbed his neck. "So, what do you think?"

"I like it," Beekman said. "I met one of our neighbors. Moxie LaMoca. He used to be a boxer. He lives in number one. He's a singing waiter." He'd let his father discover the rest for himself.

Leo nodded. "Your room okay?"

"Great," Beekman said.

"Have everything you need?"

"I do," Beekman said. He didn't see how the present set of circumstances could be improved upon.

"I was thinking that you're old enough to have some privacy," Leo said. "I was thinking I wouldn't come up here unless I'm invited."

"Even when I'm not here?" Beekman asked. "You won't come up even then?"

"Even when you're not here," Leo said. "You'll have to take care of it. Keep it clean."

"I'll take care of it," Beekman said. "And I won't come into your room unless you invite me."

"Sounds like a deal," Leo said. "We'll do some grocery shopping later. We'll get takeout for dinner."

"Pizza?"

"Pepperoni on my half," Leo said.

"My half plain," Beekman said.

The doorbell rang and Leo stood without thinking and smacked his head against the ceiling. *Whap!* He yelled a blue streak and jumped around on one foot and held his head where it hurt and banged it on the ceiling a second time.

Beekman laughed. He couldn't help himself.

"Next time we have a talk," Leo said, "we'll have it downstairs."

The doorbell rang again.

# 6

## Fernanda

"I thought this might come in handy," the woman at the door said. She handed Leo a small round cake with a carrot on top. Her voice was husky, a warmer, softer version of Beekman's rasp.

"Fernanda Bloom," the woman said, "your neighbor in number two." She was wearing a painter's hat that was speckled with fresh red paint, a paint-smeared T-shirt with a pair of giant red lips on the front, and high-tops. An eagle in flight was tattooed on her left arm.

"Leo O'Day," Leo said. "Thanks for the cake."

"I'm painting my living room," Fernanda Bloom said by way of explaining her appearance.

"It's a nice shade of red," Leo said.

Beekman could tell that his father was impressed with Fernanda Bloom, which was unusual because Leo wasn't impressed by much. But then, Fernanda Bloom was nothing less than miraculous. Her hair was as coal-black as his father's. Her eyes were a deep, dark brown. When she smiled it was like the sun coming out from behind a cloud.

"If anything needs fixing, let me know," Fernanda said. "I'm good with tools and I own a bunch of them." She looked Leo up and down with interest.

"I'll do that," Leo said. "I'll let you know. Right now everything is aces. Isn't it, son of mine?" He turned to look at Beekman, who was sitting on the stairs, halfway up.

"Everything is aces," Beekman said, sliding down a couple of steps to be closer. His eyes were glued to Fernanda's astounding presence.

"I'm Fernanda," she said.

"I'm Beekman," he said, his voice on the verge of a croak. He cleared his throat and hoped for the best as he made his way down the rest of the stairs, where he offered his hand in greeting.

"You're extremely good-looking," Beekman said. "I hope you don't mind me saying so."

"You can call me extremely good-looking anytime

you like," Fernanda said. "I think you're cute and I think we're simpatico. If you need anything, let me know. I'm almost always home."

"I will," Beekman said. "If I need anything, I'll be right over."

"You too," Fernanda said to Leo. "Any questions, knock on my door."

Beekman stood at his father's side and watched Fernanda Bloom walk across the cobblestones to her house. She turned before going in and locked eyes with Leo and smiled. Then she was closing the door behind her in a movement that was as swift and graceful as a ballet dancer's.

"She likes you," Leo said.

"Yeah," Beekman responded, "but not as much as she likes you."

# 7

## Beek the Geek

Getting to school on time required getting up early. Chance Academy was a long way from Nutting Court. But Beekman wasn't going to complain. Not about that. Not about anything. Not even about the bowl of steaming hot groats that Leo served him for breakfast. Beekman had hoped that the groats would get lost in the move. No such luck. Leo gave him ten dollars to start the week. He had a pass for the bus and subway. His backpack was loaded with books. His shoes were shined, his pants were pressed, and his necktie had a firm knot in it.

Beekman and his father stood together in front of the mirror. Leo looked particularly handsome this morning in his midnight-blue suit. They sang a chorus of "Side by Side" and danced a little dance to go with it.

"If vaudeville wasn't dead," Leo said, "we could be an act."

"We are an act," Beekman said.

Beekman left for school by himself. Leo had phone calls to make before he started his day of meetings. What his father did and where he did it remained largely a mystery. Beekman looked up and down the cobblestone alley with a sense of proprietorship. The fountain gurgled. The maple tree's branches stirred. He was aware of being watched and caught a glimpse of Sergio West looking at him from behind a curtain in number four. And he was certain that somebody in number three was watching him as well. Either Larry or Edna Biggs.

He headed for Third Avenue. He could walk to Grand Central Terminal, take the shuttle to Times Square, take the uptown local to Eighty-sixth Street, and walk the two blocks to school. Or, he could take the bus up Third Avenue to Eighty-sixth, take the crosstown bus to Columbus Avenue, and walk from there. He liked the bus. He hated the subway. He'd spoken the truth when he told the mighty McCann that he couldn't stand being underground. The bus was slower. Much slower. He'd be able to do some of the homework he was supposed to have done over the weekend.

Math on the bus wasn't possible. His pencil kept jumping off the paper. Latin was out of the question anywhere. He read a chapter of American history, then began *Frankenstein*, which was what they were reading in English class. He looked briefly at his science book. Mr. Keen had said that they'd begin dissecting soon. He hadn't said what they'd be dissecting. Not that it mattered. Beekman hated the whole idea of cutting things open and looking inside them.

The bus to Eighty-sixth Street took a long time. So did the bus that took him crosstown through Central Park. He ran from Columbus Avenue to school. He ran through the huge front doors and across the marble floor, slipping and sliding across its polished surface. He flew through the door into chapel just as it was being closed. He spotted his class and saw Marcus Peavy waving at him and making room and saw that there was nowhere else to sit. Sweating, sucking in as much air as he could without drawing everybody's attention, Beekman wedged himself onto the bench next to Marcus Peavy and turned his attention to the stage, where he saw the mighty McCann scowling down at him.

"You were almost late," Marcus Peavy whispered from the side of his mouth. "You're lucky I saved you a seat."

Everything was brief; the singing and the reading, which was delivered by a sixth former and was about doing things for other people. The mighty McCann announced that elections for student council would be held in three weeks, and that he would be appointing, as he did each year, an at-large member to both the upper- and lower-school councils. His eyes fixed on Beekman, the mighty McCann reminded the assembled that promptness was a virtue. He sent the boys of Chance Academy on their way.

It was in math that Beekman became "Beek the geek." Not that it was the first time in his life that he'd been called that. *Beek the geek* just seemed to roll off some kids' tongues. Mr. Gno stepped out of the room for a minute with the admonition that everybody keep a lid on it. As soon as he was gone, the big round kid in front of Beekman turned and asked him if Beekman was his real name.

"Is it Beekman with two *e*'s?" the kid asked. "Or is it with an *a*? Such as in a bird's beak. Such as in eagle beak. Or is it simply Beek the geek?"

Beekman shrugged it off.

"Beek the geek," the kid said again.

"It's Beekman with two *e*'s," Beekman said. "As in Beek the geek, which is fine with me. Or you could call me Beek the freak. That would be okay too." He could feel a croak working its way up his throat.

"Way to go," Marcus Peavy said. He was sitting a row away.

Beekman turned in his chair. He didn't want this Marcus Peavy getting any ideas. "Marcus the carcass," he said. An enormous croak followed.

"I thought I told you to keep it buttoned up, Mr. O'Day," Mr. Gno said as he returned.

"Yes, sir," Beekman said, way too loud.

A pained expression creased Mr. Gno's well-lined face as he moved to the blackboard and began writing. "Perhaps Mr. O'Day will help us solve a word problem," he said. "Step up here, Mr. O'Day."

Beekman hated word problems. He hated getting up in front of the class. Any class. Most of all a class where he had no idea what was going on.

"A train leaves the station in Chicago and heads for New York City traveling at a speed of one hundred seventy-five miles an hour," Mr. Gno said as he wrote. "Another train leaves New York City at exactly the same time and heads for Chicago at one hundred fifty miles an hour . . ."

Mr. Gno droned on. Beekman didn't hear a word of

it. He was thinking about how much he liked traveling by train. He liked the motion and the sound and being able to sit very still and watch mile after mile of the world pass by. He had no idea when and where Mr. Gno's two trains would meet.

After math came Latin. On Mondays, Mr. Nussbaum spoke only Latin in class. For the entire time. Immersion is what he called it. Absorption by osmosis. If you couldn't answer his questions in Latin you got an F for the day. Beekman held his own in history and English. Marcus Peavy caught up with him in the lunch line.

"Marcus the carcass," Marcus Peavy said. "That's a good one."

"You like being insulted?" Beekman asked.

"That's not an insult," Marcus Peavy said. "Marcus the carcass is an honorable name. A name for a member of Caesar's senate. A name for a Shakespeare play."

Beekman ordered the cheese ravioli. Marcus Peavy ordered the same. Beekman sat at an empty table. Marcus Peavy sat next to him.

"How come you started school later than the rest of us?" Marcus Peavy asked, tucking his napkin into his shirt collar. He saw Beekman staring at the napkin. "I have a tendency to get food on my clothes," he said.

**57**

"I just did," Beekman responded. He turned his attention to lunch. The ravioli had an industrial aftertaste.

"It's very expensive here," Marcus Peavy said. "Unless you're on a scholarship. Are you on a scholarship?"

Beekman shook his head. He was watching a tall, rangy kid with a permanent smirk attached to his face move toward him. The kid was giving him a hard looking over.

"That's Searle," Marcus Peavy whispered. "Whatever you do, don't make him mad at you."

"You were late for chapel this morning," Searle said when he reached Beekman's table.

Beekman looked up at Searle. "Almost late," he said.

"You were late starting school," Searle said.

"You got me there," Beekman said.

"You some kind of hardship case?" Searle asked. "You special?"

"I am special," Beekman said. "I have leprosy." He held out his hand for Searle to shake. "It's nice to meet you."

Searle took a fast step back.

Marcus Peavy laughed, then bit his hand to stop himself.

"Leprosy's not funny," Beekman said.

Searle glared at Beekman. "You think you're pretty smart," he said.

"Not as smart as you," Beekman said. "You must be the smartest kid in the whole school. You must be a genius."

Searle held a fist up in front of Beekman's face. "I'll see you later," he said.

Beekman watched Searle join a group of second formers. He knew trouble when he saw it.

"You're in for it now," Marcus said. "I'd try to stay out of his way if I were you."

After lunch, Señor Gomez rattled on double-speed in Spanish, then gave a pop quiz. Beekman figured he was lucky if he got half of the questions right. Dr. Tarter showed a video of his summer trip to Israel. Mr. Keen said they'd begin dissecting chicken feet as a means of studying the human hand in a few days.

After science class, Searle dragged Beekman to the basement, pummeled him for having a big mouth, then locked him in the boiler room. Marcus Peavy let him out.

At three-thirty, Beekman was back on the street, on the run, with Marcus Peavy in pursuit.

# 8

## Marcus Peavy

"Wait for me!" Marcus Peavy was running as fast as he could.

Beekman was a block ahead of him on the way to the bus stop at Eighty-sixth Street, hoping that a bus would pull up just as he got there, open its doors, take him into its belly, and be gone by the time Marcus Peavy arrived. Beekman had had enough of Marcus Peavy for one day.

There wasn't a bus to be seen. Beekman looked back and saw Marcus Peavy cross the street, bobbing and weaving his way through traffic like a raft in white water. Marcus Peavy was persistent. Beekman would give him that.

"Boy, that was some run," Marcus said, barely able to speak because he was breathing so hard. "I don't think I could have made it one more block. Thanks for waiting."

Beekman looked impatiently for a bus, as though by willing it he could make one appear. Better yet, he thought, when he turned around, Marcus Peavy would be gone.

"It's a good thing I saw Searle lock you in the boiler room," Marcus said. "Otherwise you might still be in there."

"Thanks," Beekman said. He hated being indebted to anybody.

"Hoffsteader, he's in second form," Marcus said, "Hoffsteader said that last year Searle picked on the same kid until the kid couldn't take it anymore and quit school."

A bus showed itself. Beekman could separate himself from Marcus Peavy once they were onboard. They flashed their passes and Beekman charged to the back looking for a single seat. He found one by a window, next to an extremely large man whose presence on the aisle would surely deter Marcus Peavy from getting too close. Marcus grabbed the nearby pole as the bus pulled away. The large man pushed himself to his feet to get off at the next stop. Marcus slipped into the seat next to Beek-man.

"Where do you live?" Marcus asked.

"Downtown," Beekman said. Marcus Peavy was like having gum stuck to your shoe.

"Where downtown?"

"Below Forty-second Street," Beekman said. "Down there."

"Where down there?"

"Nutting Court," Beekman said.

"I never heard of Nutting Court. Where is it?"

"Downtown, I told you. East side. Now quit bugging me."

"I live at Eighty-ninth and Park," Marcus said. "You want to come over?"

"No," Beekman said with the kind of finality that would ordinarily put a stop to a conversation.

"It could be today or any day," Marcus said. "It doesn't matter what day it is."

"I'm under strict orders to come straight home from school," Beekman said. "I'm under house arrest. I can't go anywhere."

"What did you do?" Marcus's eyes widened.

"I killed somebody for asking too many questions," Beekman said.

Marcus laughed. "You're the funniest person I've

ever met," he said. "You could come on the weekend. I could have my mother call your mother."

"There's just my father," Beekman said. He hadn't meant to divulge any information about himself, and now Marcus Peavy knew where he lived and that he didn't have a mother. "I'm not coming to your apartment," Beekman said, "so just shut up about it." He looked out the window. They were making their way through Central Park. The leaves would start changing color soon. Then they'd start falling off the trees and he'd be able to jump in them. He loved jumping in leaves.

"I wasn't laughing at leprosy, you know," Marcus said. "I'd like that understood. I was laughing at the way you got Searle so shook up."

Beekman ignored him.

"Actually, leprosy is called Hansen's disease. After Dr. Armauer Hansen, who discovered some of its secrets. He was Norwegian. It's caused by the bacillus *Mycobacterium leprae*. How it's transmitted is still mostly a mystery. It's capable of producing all sorts of deformities. People can lose their noses and hands. It spreads most rapidly in crowded and unsanitary conditions. In the United States you can find leprosariums in Louisiana, Hawaii, and New York City. It can be treated, but there's no cure."

"How come you know all that?" Beekman asked, nearly mesmerized by the flow of information coming from his classmate's lips.

"I remember everything I see and hear and read," Marcus said. "I can't help it. I was born that way. Maybe I could come to Nutting Court sometime to visit you."

"I don't think so," Beekman said, still stunned by the depth of Marcus Peavy's knowledge.

"Sure, I understand," Marcus said. "You think I'm a loser." He stood. Park Avenue was the next stop. "I'll bet you don't know that a lot of people call our school Last Chance Academy. I'll bet you don't know why."

Beekman stared at Marcus Peavy. He had no idea.

"A lot of people think it's a school for losers, that's why. Chance is for the socially and behaviorally challenged. The ones who don't fit in anywhere else. The rejected. I'll bet you didn't know any of that." Marcus ran for the door. "I'll see you tomorrow," he said with a hopeful smile.

Beekman watched Marcus Peavy become smaller and smaller as the bus drove off, until he couldn't see him anymore. Was it true? Was it really Last Chance Academy? That would explain why he'd been accepted so easily. He was going to a school for losers.

# 9

## Cocoa and Cookies

Beekman knocked at the red door. He was excited about seeing Fernanda Bloom. The thought of spending the rest of the afternoon with her cheered him up considerably. He wanted to forget about Last Chance Academy and Marcus Peavy. He'd ask Fernanda if she wanted to go out for a soda maybe, or they could just hang out at her place. He didn't care. He had business to discuss. Pertaining to his father. He knocked again, then added a long push of the bell. She wasn't home.

He swallowed his disappointment and headed back across the alley. He'd try her later. He felt a tug, as though somebody were pulling at him. He stopped and looked around. He saw Loomis Garcia looking at him through a window in number six. He felt the tug again. His gaze settled on the purple door. He felt himself moving toward it, drawn like a night-flying insect to a light. He found himself knocking on it, wondering why.

The door opened. Before him stood a large, soft fairy godmother of a woman in all her purple majesty. She was wearing a long flowing purple gown. Her hair was frosted purple, with specks of purple glitter in it, stars all atwinkle in a lavender galaxy of curls. Her shoes were purple.

"You're all purple," Beekman said.

"And you're Beekman O'Day," she said. "And you know who I am."

"Madam de Campo," Beekman said.

"Exactly correct," she said. "Come in. Come in." Her voice was a breathless whisper. "I just have cocoa on the stove." She headed for the kitchen. "Close the door and make yourself comfortable."

Beekman entered Madam de Campo's living room. The curtains and carpets and furniture fabrics and walls were all some variation of the color purple. The ceiling glowed like lilacs on a sunny day. There were violets everywhere. Even the air seemed purple, the result of purple-tinted lightbulbs. He looked at his hands. They appeared to be purple too.

"Why is everything purple?" Beekman asked, turning in a slow circle.

"Why is the grass green and the sky blue?" Madam de Campo responded from the kitchen. "Why is the moon made of cheese?"

"It's not made of cheese," Beekman said.

"But maybe the center is," she said. "Who knows? Maybe the moon is a cosmic golf ball that's been lost in the rough. Who knows?"

Madam de Campo emerged from the kitchen with two large mugs of steaming cocoa, each with a single marshmallow floating at its surface, each marshmallow supporting a small paper flag atop a toothpick. There was also a plate of thin, golden cookies that were lightly dusted with powdered sugar, which to Beekman looked like snow. She set the tray down on the purple coffee table and arranged herself on the purple couch.

"Sit wherever you like," she said. "I prefer sitting near the cookies myself." She lifted a cookie daintily from the plate and took a bite.

"What kind of cookies are they?" Beekman asked. He liked to know what he was eating.

"Lemon cookies," she said with a dreamy expression on her face. "Not too tart. Not too sweet. Just exactly right."

"What flag is that?" Beekman asked.

"The tricolor. The flag of France."

"Why is the French flag floating in the cocoa?"

"I also have one stuck in a bar of soap that floats in the bathtub," she said. She took another nibble of her cookie. She sipped at her cocoa.

"The temperature of the cocoa is just exactly perfect," Madam de Campo said. "This is the exactly correct time to drink it."

Beekman selected a cookie and took his mug of cocoa and sat at the far end of the couch. He glanced at Madam de Campo, who was taking another bite of her cookie. He freed his marshmallow from its flag and ate it. He filled his mouth with cocoa and let it sit there while the chocolate coated his teeth and gums and tongue. He swallowed. It was the richest, most chocolate cocoa he'd ever had. He took another drink of it, then another. The cookie dissolved in his mouth.

"I like purple," Madam de Campo said when her cookie was consumed. "I like France. Especially Paris. I like cocoa and cookies." She wiped a pebble of a crumb from the corner of her mouth.

"One should allow oneself to like exactly what one

likes and to do exactly what one likes to do," she said. "When one can. Don't you agree?"

"I do," Beekman said between a bite of cookie and a mouthful of cocoa.

Madam de Campo dunked a cookie into her cocoa. "The cookie absorbs the chocolate," she said. "It adds dimension to the taste of the lemon." She closed her eyes and ate the cookie, then turned to him. "So, you're Beekman O'Day."

"I am," Beekman said.

"You're in the seventh grade," she said.

"I am," he said. "Except where I go it's called first form."

"That would be Chance Academy," she said.

He wondered how she knew. He hadn't been accepted when his father had found this place.

"Old-fashioned, but excellent," she said. "It may not prepare you for the technological revolution, but it will prepare you for life."

"How do you know about the school I'm going to?" Beekman asked.

"My uncle Howard attended Chance," Madam de Campo said. "He called it Last Chance, but it wasn't really. It was and is a proper school for young gentlemen."

"I'm not sure how I'll fit in," he said.

"You'll fit in fine," she said. "Try dunking your cookie."

He did. It was delicious. He wondered how much cocoa and how many cookies he could consume before he got sick.

"You should throw a get-acquainted party," Madam de Campo said, taking yet another cookie. "Nothing fancy. On a Sunday afternoon. Soon. That's when everybody can come."

"I'll do it," Beekman said. It was how he could bring his father and Fernanda together. His eye caught the large round bulge beneath the purple cloth that covered the purple table in the middle of the room.

"My crystal ball," Madam de Campo said.

"Are you a fortune-teller?" Beekman asked, amazed by such a prospect.

"Perhaps one day we'll look into the future together," she said.

Beekman was excited, then concerned. What would she tell him about Nutting Court and Chance Academy and his father's promises?

"Maybe it's better to wait and see what happens," Beekman said, taking another cookie.

"Either way it's the future," Madam de Campo said. "It's good to have you here at last, Beekman O'Day."

# 10

## How the Day Went

"Beekman is a stupid name."

"It's a great name."

Beekman and his father were standing in front of the mirror.

"I hate the name Beekman," Beekman said. "I don't know why you gave it to me in the first place."

"I've told you many times, son of mine," Leo said, "that the moment I saw you I said to myself, this boy's name is Beekman."

"Hooey," Beekman said.

"I considered hooey," Leo said. "Hooey O'Day. I thought Beekman sounded better."

"Beekman is a hotel name," Beekman said. "A name

for an office building. The Beekman Towers. It's the name of a car. Get better mileage with this year's Beekman."

"Beekman is a distinguished name," Leo said, refolding his silk pocket handkerchief. "Someday when you're president of the United States, you'll thank me."

"I don't want to be president of the United States. I don't want to be president of anything. I'm a loser."

"When did that happen?"

"Since I started going to a school for losers. Last Chance Academy is what it's called. Ulysses S. Chance must have been a loser too."

Leo squatted so he could look his son in the eye. "You think I'm a loser?"

"No," Beekman said.

"You think I'd send my one and only boy to a school for losers?"

Beekman hesitated.

"There may be kids at Chance who think they're losers," Leo said, "but believe me, Headmaster McCann wouldn't let a loser in. Not for a minute."

Beekman considered his father's words. Maybe Chance wasn't for losers. Maybe it was and Leo didn't know it. Searle was a loser. He wasn't sure about Marcus Peavy. He wasn't so sure about himself.

"Beekman O'Day is not a loser," Leo said. "Beekman O'Day does not go to a school for losers."

Beekman wasn't happy this morning. Not about anything. He didn't like the way he looked. He didn't like what he was wearing. He didn't care for his raspy voice.

"I know Beekman was my mother's last name before she married you," Beekman said, "but I don't want it and I don't know why I have to keep it. She's dead and I didn't even know her and I don't see how it can matter anymore."

"Of course you knew her," Leo said. "You just don't remember her."

"When I grow up I'm going to change it," Beekman said.

"I hope not."

"Why'd she make you call me that anyway?"

"She didn't make me. I did it all by myself. And that's enough about your name. We've got a big day ahead of us. Chance Academy awaits. I'm working on a big deal. You wouldn't believe how big if I told you, which I'm not because I don't have enough of the pieces put together yet. This could be the one."

"Go get 'em, Pop," Beekman said.

"You too, my one and only son," Leo said.

Beekman didn't want to go to school. But he went.

He wanted to be late. But he wasn't. Everything went smoothly buswise and otherwise, and he actually got to chapel two minutes early. Once again Marcus Peavy had saved him a seat. He took it so Marcus wouldn't make a scene. He'd find a different place tomorrow.

In science class they began dissecting chicken feet. Marcus volunteered to be Beekman's partner.

"The reason we are dissecting these chicken feet," Mr. Keen said to the class while holding one up for everybody to see, "is so we can better understand how our fingers work." Mr. Keen sounded wistful, like a man who'd once led a far more interesting life. "It's the next best thing to cutting open a human hand. Unless we have a volunteer for that." Mr. Keen laughed. Beekman figured it must be science humor, so he laughed with him. To help him out. The rest of the class erupted into a loud chorus of chicken sounds, which caused Mr. Keen to wince.

"The task at hand, so to speak," Mr. Keen continued, doing his best to ignore the clucking, "is to make careful, clean cuts along your chicken foot as I've done here . . ." He pulled back the dissected skin to reveal the tendons. More clucks. With a couple of *cock-a-doodle-doo*s thrown in for good measure. "You'll carefully lift the tendons and you'll pull on them gently." Mr. Keen demonstrated. One of the toes on the foot moved. "Chicken toes approximate human fingers in how they move."

Beekman hated the idea of dissecting a chicken foot.

"I'll make the first cut," Marcus said. "We'll be world-famous surgeons performing the world's most difficult operation."

"You can do all the cutting if it makes you happy," Beekman said.

"Be careful with those scalpels," Mr. Keen said. "I don't want to see any blood."

Beekman watched as Marcus made an incision in the pickled chicken foot. It was a former body part. Something a live chicken once used to get around on. Without the chicken attached to it, Beekman thought it looked a lot like the hand of some creature from another solar system. A claw that could rip your face off with a single swipe. What if there was a planet out there somewhere where the chickens were in charge? What if they dissected human hands to see how chicken toes worked?

"How's it coming along, Beekman?" Mr. Keen asked. Unlike the other teachers at Chance, Mr. Keen called his students by their first names.

"It's going hunky-dory," Beekman said. "Dr. Peavy here is performing the surgery."

"Beekman eats chicken feet," the big round boy, whose name was Wibble, yelled out from across the room.

"Beekman sucks the skin off chicken toes," Foyle yelled.

"Beekman bites the heads off live chickens," Hanser said.

"A person who bites the heads off live chickens is called a Beekman," Bates said.

"A person who bites the heads off live chickens is called a geek," Mr. Keen said, correcting Bates.

"Beek the geek," Wibble yelled.

"Quiet!" Mr. Keen shouted, his voice going shrill. "I'll be around to inspect everybody's work. You'd better be ready."

"Hey! Look what mine can do!" Wibble pulled on all three tendons of his chicken foot at once, then pulled the toes back up, then pulled the tendons again, creating the illusion that the chicken foot was waving goodbye.

Hackney pulled on a tendon, and a toe popped up and he pretended he was picking his nose with it.

"A chicken hitchhiking," Foyle yelled as he popped up the "thumb" of the chicken foot and jerked it back and forth.

Mr. Keen pleaded for order.

"Peace," Carnaby yelled, pulling on two tendons and producing the *V* sign.

"Please," Mr. Keen implored. "Settle down. Fun is fun, but we have work to do. Please."

It was too little too late. The class was out of control. Beekman had had enough of his idiot classmates and their name-calling.

"How about this!" Beekman screamed, his voice croaking like a swamp full of frogs. "Here's what I think of all of you." He grabbed the chicken foot away from Marcus and held it up and pulled on the middle tendon and the corresponding chicken digit shot up into the air. "I hate this school," Beekman said as he walked out of the room.

He considered cutting the rest of the day, but he was already in enough trouble. Mr. Keen would report him to the mighty McCann, who would breathe fire and brimstone on him. He climbed the stairs to the fourth floor. Mr. Jack was teaching a class in personal hygiene. The locker room would be empty. He pushed open the swinging door and was grabbed and spun around and punched in the stomach.

"Good to see you, Beekman," Searle said, like he'd been expecting him.

Beekman gasped for air. He heard Searle laughing.

"Thanks for stopping by," Searle said, pushing Beekman back out the door.

At lunch, Wibble, Foyle, and Carnaby sat at his table and congratulated him for breaking up science class. Two minutes after he'd walked out, Mr. Keen, in tears, dismissed them. Beekman didn't want their congratulations. He took his fried chicken and mashed potatoes—which he'd ordered only because the other choice was beef stew, and who knew what they put in that—to another table. A minute later, Marcus Peavy walked by.

"I'm not sitting with you today," Marcus said. "You upset Mr. Keen and I didn't get to finish dissecting our chicken foot. I wanted to learn about fingers."

Beekman returned the fried chicken uneaten. He couldn't stop thinking about its missing parts. He found Mr. Keen in his classroom sorting through chicken feet, trying to salvage what he could of them for another attempt.

"I don't know what got into me," Beekman said from the doorway. "I'm generally not like that. I mean, I hardly ever make trouble for anybody but myself." He took a few steps into the room.

"I expected more from you, Beekman," Mr. Keen said. He looked up. His eyes were red-rimmed.

"I'm sorry," Beekman said. He wondered why Mr. Keen would expect anything from him. "How can you teach here?" he asked, moving the rest of the way to the lab table, where Mr. Keen was doing his sorting. "Everybody here is a loser, including me."

"There are no losers," Mr. Keen said, "only lost people." He pushed a box of chicken feet in Beekman's direction. "See if any of these can be used again."

Beekman spent the lunch hour sorting through chicken feet with Mr. Keen, who did not report him to the mighty McCann. He attended his afternoon classes without incident. His stomach remained tender to the touch. Searle would have to be dealt with.

Marcus Peavy followed him to the bus stop and sat next to him on the bus and acted like nothing had happened in science class. He talked the whole way to Eighty-sixth Street and Park Avenue about the possibility of life on Mars.

# 11

## The Party

At precisely four o'clock in the afternoon on the Sunday appointed, the residents of Nutting Court left their houses and made their way to number eight, with the rose-colored door, which was open in anticipation of their arrival. Beekman greeted them and introduced them to his father.

Madam de Campo was a vision of purpleness. She radiated purple. Leo smiled his most charming smile, the one that revealed the dimple, and kissed her hand.

"Enchanted," Leo said.

Madam de Campo handed him a tin of lemon cookies. "Eat them while they're fresh," she said. "It's a pleasure to finally meet you, Leo."

"The pleasure is mine," Leo said.

"We're happy you're here," she said, smiling at Beekman.

Moxie LaMoca came dressed as the famous old movie star Mae West. "Why don't you come up and see me sometime," Moxie said to Leo in a throaty approximation of Mae West's voice. "You can peel me a grape." Moxie handed Leo a jar of his homemade salsa. "I do an excellent Mae West, but nobody remembers her anymore. Nobody appreciates history in this country. If you're not on TV, you don't exist. You got a great kid here, Leo." Moxie wandered off in his slinky dress to join Madam de Campo at the cheese platter.

Edna and Larry Biggs brought a houseplant. She was tall and thin. He was short and square. She was a bus driver. He painted billboards. They hugged Leo and gave Beekman a knowing smile.

Loomis Garcia presented Leo with a large brown paper bag that had a blue ribbon tied around it.

"Very kind," Leo said, examining the bag.

"It's Zoo Doo," Loomis said. "The five-pound gift size. Nothing like it to make the flowers grow."

"How is the Zoo Doo business these days?" Leo asked.

"Never ending," Loomis said. He shook Beekman's hand. "Good to see you again," he said.

When Loomis was gone, Beekman explained that Zoo Doo was elephant poop, and that Loomis was in charge of the Zoo Doo program at the zoo.

"Elephants are herbivores," Beekman said, "so their poop doesn't stink. Not after it ages. Loomis says they have a mountain of it out there. He says elephants can unload a couple hundred pounds at a time."

"That's probably all I need to know about elephant poop," Leo said. "People actually buy this stuff?"

"Loomis says they buy it by the truckload. Loomis says that there's no doo like Zoo Doo."

Minnie and Manfried Mumm, who were both four feet eight inches tall, brought a loaf of bread, a candle, and a jar of honey.

"The candle is so you'll always have light," Minnie said.

"The bread is so you'll always have something to eat," Manfried said.

"The honey is so that your lives will always be sweet," they said together.

The Mumms were immaculately attired in formal dress. It was hard to tell how old they were.

"They run a formerly owned formal-wear shop," Beekman said to Leo when they were gone.

Sergio West showed up in a wrinkled linen suit, wrinkled shirt, and sneakers. He needed a shave and a haircut. "How you doing?" he asked Beekman in an accent that was pure Boston.

"Good," Beekman said.

"How you doing?" Sergio West asked Leo.

"Good," Leo said. "Glad you could make it."

"Glad I could make it," Sergio said. He handed Leo a bottle of red wine that was so encrusted with dust you couldn't read the label. "It's ready to drink," he said. He turned to Beekman. "Come around. We can do some more talking."

"He's a writer," Beekman told Leo. "His great-great-grandfather was a slave."

That left Fernanda, who moved through the doorway at that very moment. She was wearing a key-lime-pie shade of green dress, and there was a daisy fixed in her hair. She kissed Beekman on the cheek, then turned her attention to Leo. Her housewarming gift was a majestic coconut cake with a lighted sparkler on top of it.

Beekman offered his guests cheese and crackers, raw vegetables, and chips and dip. He filled glasses with juice, club soda, and wine. It was, after all, his party. He was the host. He'd decided what to serve. He'd decided to do the serving. He wanted his father to know these people. Most of all Fernanda, whom he was happy to see at his father's side. He caught her eye and she smiled at him, as though they were partners in some secret plot that was going well. It was perfectly clear to him that she and his father were destined to get married. If they didn't understand that yet, he'd have to help them.

After the other guests had left, each of them telling Beekman what a good time they'd had and how much they'd enjoyed meeting his father, Beekman suggested that Leo walk Fernanda back to her house.

"My father is going to walk you home" is how Beekman put it.

"You heard the man," Leo said.

"I heard him," Fernanda said. She kissed Beekman. "Thanks for inviting me."

"Thanks for coming," Beekman managed to rasp. He watched them walk across the alley in the warm, fuzzy light of early evening. They walked slowly, as though trying to prolong the journey. At her door they turned to each other and talked.

A good beginning, Beekman thought.

# 12

## Up a Rope

He finally succeeded. He arrived at school at one minute past nine. He was locked out of chapel. Inside was an empty space next to Marcus Peavy. The one Marcus saved for him every day. The mighty McCann was, at that very moment, looking at the empty space. The mighty McCann would call him into the inner sanctum later in the day. So what? Life would go on. Nothing would change. Arriving at Chance Academy one minute late wasn't going to make the world a worse place than it already was. He saw Miss Haymaker looking at him from the doorway to her office.

"Good morning, Miss Haymaker," Beekman said. "I'm late."

"You're a funny boy," Miss Haymaker said. "Head-master will want to see you later."

"I'm available at his convenience," Beekman said. He made his way to the second floor. He took a long drink from the water fountain. He put his books in his locker. He walked backwards up the stairs to the third floor. He inspected the classrooms of the upper school. They looked the same as the ones below. They smelled the same. Did nothing magical happen when you moved from one floor to the next?

He made his way to the fourth floor, to the empty locker room where he changed for physical education. He hated physical education. In navy blue shorts and a white T-shirt, he picked up a basketball and dribbled it up and down the gym floor, then started shooting baskets. He'd missed twenty-seven shots in a row when Mr. Jack and the rest of his class showed up.

"I'm *so* sorry," Mr. Jack said. "We're obliged to have a *test* today." Mr. Jack's suit was just a little too small. The pants were too short. So were the sleeves. His necktie bore the vestiges of many hastily eaten meals.

The class moaned.

"I don't want to be *here* any more than you do," Mr. Jack said. "I was hired to teach government studies. Nobody told me *this* went with it."

"He's been doing *this* for thirty years," Marcus whispered to Beekman.

"Thank you *so* much for talking," Mr. Jack said to Marcus Peavy. "You missed chapel this morning, Mr. O'Day, so you can be *first* to *climb* the *rope*."

"My knee hurts," Beekman said.

"I'm *so* sorry," Mr. Jack said. "See how far you can get using your *hands*."

Beekman stared at the end of the rope, which dangled some seven feet above him. He wasn't sure he could jump high enough to grab it, never mind climb it.

"I would be ever so *grateful* if you started *now*," Mr. Jack said.

Beekman jumped as high as he could and just caught hold of the bottom of the rope.

"Mr. O'Day will *now demonstrate* the finer points of rope climbing," Mr. Jack said to the class. "*Hand* over *hand*," he said to Beekman.

Beekman gave it everything he had. He climbed, hand over hand, and pulled his legs up behind him and wrapped them around the rope. He hung there like a koala bear on a vine.

"Like *most* things in *life*, Mr. O'Day," Mr. Jack said, "the task requires some effort."

Beekman looked up. The top seemed a mile away.

"Our bodies need *work*," Mr. Jack said. "A strong mind without a strong *body* is *half a loaf*."

Beekman imagined himself hanging precariously to a lifeline on the side of a sheer cliff. He had to climb it to save his life. He had to hurry before the line snapped and he plunged to a certain death.

"You have *sixty seconds* to complete the task, Mr. O'Day, then it will be somebody else's *turn*. As it stands, I'll give you *ten* points out of a *hundred* for being able to reach the rope *at all*. There are *nine* more events."

Beekman wanted to climb the rope with one hand, then swing out on it, do a triple somersault, and land on his feet. Instead he let go and fell to the mat. *Thud!* Like a box falling off a shelf.

Mr. Jack shook his head sadly and lifted his clipboard to make a notation. "A *bird* could arm wrestle you to the ground," he said to Beekman.

Beekman managed eleven push-ups and twenty-one sit-ups. He lifted seventy pounds, then dropped it on the floor. He jumped up on the horse, but had a hard time getting off. He couldn't get his legs out in front of him on the rings. None of it went well. He wasn't the only one. Marcus Peavy was bigger and stronger, but uncoordinated in every way. He was a walking misfortune when it came to anything physical. Wibble got his bulk halfway up the rope. Foyle nearly ruined himself tumbling. Carnaby couldn't jump high enough to reach the top of the horse. Wu, Cornhoser, and Hackney excelled at it all.

"Thank you *so* much," Mr. Jack said to the class when it was all over. "I *can't* remember when I've spent a more enjoyable morning."

Beekman dozed off in Latin. Mr. Nussbaum hit him with a blackboard eraser. It left a large chalk mark on his head. He was rescued from having to recite the homework he hadn't done by Searle, who had messenger duty.

"Headmaster wants to see O'Day right away," Searle announced, like he was broadcasting the most important news ever heard.

"Tomorrow we continue with Caesar's invasion of Gaul," Mr. Nussbaum said to Beekman. "You'll be the first one called upon."

Beekman moved quickly past Searle into the hall. "McCann's going to have you for lunch," Searle said, "and I'm going to have what's left."

"What did I do to you?" Beekman asked, hurrying to stay ahead of Searle. "How come you're picking on me?"

"I looked over everybody in your class," Searle

said, "and I couldn't make up my mind. Peavy, Foyle . . . there were several candidates. Then you showed up."

"What's that got to do with anything?" Beekman asked, feeling Searle right behind him. "Leave me alone."

"I don't want to leave you alone," Searle said.

Beekman started running down the stairs.

Searle slapped him hard on the back of his head and Beekman stumbled forward and fell and banged his knee and elbow before he came to a stop.

"See you around," Searle said, heading back to the second floor. "Real soon."

Beekman waited until Searle was gone, then walked back and forth across the grand entry until he could manage it without limping, then presented himself to Miss Haymaker.

"He's waiting for you," Miss Haymaker said.

"Thank you, Miss Haymaker," Beekman said. "You're looking particularly lovely today." He marched into the mighty McCann's office. What was the worst that could happen? He'd get thrown out?

"Close the door, Mr. O'Day," the mighty McCann said without looking up from the file he was reading. "Then come sit here in front of me."

Beekman closed the door and sat, feeling smaller

than he already was because the desk was so big. He could just see over the top of it.

"You were late this morning," the mighty McCann said.

"No excuse," Beekman said.

The mighty McCann glanced at Beekman with surprise. "No *but*s?" he asked.

"No *but*s," Beekman said. "I was late. It was my fault."

"You've been here almost a month," the mighty McCann said. "I thought this would be a good opportunity to see how you're doing."

"I'm not doing very well," Beekman said.

The mighty McCann closed the file and studied Beekman. "It seems that Mr. Keen has high hopes for you in science. You're keeping your head above water, barely, in history, English, government studies, and philosophy. As for the rest, disaster would be too weak a word to describe your work. You're failing Latin, math, and Spanish, and Mr. Jack informs me that you may be the first student in Chance's history to fail physical education. You can do better than this, Mr. O'Day. If I didn't believe that, I wouldn't have taken you in."

"I'm a loser," Beekman said.

"That word is not part of the Chance vocabulary,"

the mighty McCann said, his voice booming with indignation.

"Last Chance Academy," Beekman said. "Everybody here is a loser." A powerful croak gathered in his throat.

"It has been the habit of some students to refer to Chance Academy as Last Chance Academy since our founding," the mighty McCann said. "It doesn't make it so. We admit young men whose promise is unfulfilled. There isn't a school in New York City that's any tougher. What do you think I should do with you?"

"Probably the best thing would be to get rid of me," Beekman said.

The mighty McCann looked at Beekman for a very long time. "Is that what you want?" he asked finally.

"It would be the best thing, wouldn't it?" Beekman responded.

"It would mean I've failed you," the mighty McCann said. "Failure isn't acceptable. Not to me. So, I'm assigning you to Saturday school. It meets every Saturday morning from nine until twelve. In Mr. Jack's room. He's the Saturday school teacher. You'll go until your grades improve. The other thing I'm going to do is appoint you to be the at-large member of the lower-school student council."

# 13

## Working Out

Beekman grunted. "Saturday school stinks," he said through his clenched teeth. He groaned. "All you do is sit there for three hours and study. You can't ask any questions. Nobody can talk. The only good thing about it was that Searle wasn't there."

"Who's Searle?" Leo asked.

Beekman and his father were at the Gramercy Fitness Center. Leo had somehow gotten his hands on a free membership. A small debt collected from somebody.

"This kid who keeps punching me," Beekman said. "He slaps me in the back of the head."

"You can't let him do that."

"I'll take care of it, Pop."

"Why is this kid picking on you?"

"Who knows?"

"Have you talked to him?"

"He likes to do all the talking."

"Is he bigger than you?"

"Yes," Beekman said. His T-shirt was soaked through to the skin with sweat. His face was bright red.

"Tell one of your teachers," Leo said. "Tell Headmaster McCann."

"That'll make it worse," Beekman said. He had the handles of the weight machine pushed out about eight inches in front of him. His arms were shaking.

"So, you're going to fight this kid Searle," Leo said.

"I don't want to fight him," Beekman said. "I just want him to stop."

"And that's why you wanted to work out?"

"Also because I failed the physical education test," Beekman said. "I have to take it again before the Christmas break." He was holding on to the weight machine's handles for dear life. "I hate Saturday school. I hate getting up early on Saturday morning. I hate taking the subway, which I have to do so I'm not late, because if I'm late they'll make me go extra Saturdays. I don't know which is worse, stupid Saturday school or stupid student council."

"What student council?"

"The mighty McCann put me on the lower-school student council."

"Congratulations."

"All we did at the first meeting was sit around a table and talk."

"It sounds to me like the school year is off to a good start."

"Very funny," Beekman said. He closed his eyes and pushed against the handles with every bit of strength he thought he had.

"Come on, son of mine," Leo urged. "You can do it. Find what you need inside."

Beekman felt his arms wobble. He thought he was losing control. The machine was going to defeat him.

"Be strong," Leo said. "Gather your forces, then let everything out at once. You can do it."

Beekman thought about Searle and the rope climb and the humiliation and, from a place he didn't know existed, he found an extra surge of power. He felt it working its way up into his arms. He felt his elbows steady. He pushed forward with a grunt that sounded like it started at his feet. He felt the handles move away from him, a steady inch at a time. Until his arms were fully extended and he could reach no farther.

"You did it!" Leo said. "My boy did it!"

Beekman opened his eyes and saw his father smiling at him.

"It was nothing," Beekman said. His arms were starting to shake again.

"Let the handles back down slowly," Leo said. "Resist their weight. Work your arms both ways."

Beekman resisted the weight as best he could, returning the handles to their resting positions with only a small bang.

"Good for you," Leo said, completing his third set of fifteen. "Very impressive."

"I'm impressed myself," Beekman said. He flexed his muscles. He felt stronger already.

"Remember today," Leo said. "It's the day you found out how deep you can dig when you have to."

# 14

## The Shaving Lesson

Steam-shrouded figures of men beneath showerheads lathered their bodies with soap and their scalps with shampoo. Beekman had his own showerhead next to his father's. He kept his back to the others as much as he could. He didn't like showing his body. He glanced about furtively, making sure not to stare. He'd seen Leo without his clothes on plenty of times when they were using the bathroom together, but he'd never been in the company of a group of naked men. He was curious about what he might look like someday. A few were gray atop their heads and on their chests and between their legs. Most were at the peak of their strength and masculinity. A pride of young male lions.

He listened to their voices ricocheting off the tile walls and felt the hot water beating against his body and heard the slap of skin being washed and felt part of a brotherhood.

"You'll be sore in the morning," Leo said. "After a few more workouts, that won't happen anymore. You did good out there."

Beekman felt a rush of pleasure.

"Fighting won't solve your problems," Leo said. "You have to be smarter than this kid. Figure him out. Get his number."

"I'll try," Beekman said. He didn't hold out much hope that anything he said would get rid of Searle. "Can I ask you a question?"

"Ask me two," Leo said.

"There's this dance coming up I have to go to. The whole lower school has to go."

"What's the problem?"

"Besides not wanting to go, I don't do very well talking to girls. And I'm not exactly the world's best dancer."

"We'll take care of the dancing," Leo said, "but I don't understand the other part. Why would an engaging guy like you have trouble talking to a girl?"

"I haven't done much of it," Beekman said. "I could use some advice."

"You see a girl you like," Leo said, "you go up to her and introduce yourself. You ask her to dance. You ask her some questions about herself. But nothing personal. Find out what interests her. Tell her a little about yourself. But not too much. Better to listen than to talk."

"I'm no good at any of that," Beekman said.

"Be a gentleman," Leo said. "Be Beekman O'Day."

Beekman dried himself with a huge white terry towel, then wrapped a fresh one around himself the way he saw his father do it. He had to wrap the towel around himself twice. Tucked together just beneath his armpits, it still dragged on the floor. He followed Leo to the row of sinks and mirrors and watched him take a can of shaving cream from the shelf and a disposable razor from a glass bowl that was filled with them.

"You should shave when your whiskers are soft," Leo said. He looked at his son's reflection in the mirror. "Like right after a shower."

Leo applied shaving cream to the sides of his face and to his neck and chin and above his upper lip. "Soaping your face with warm water works too," he said. "Let the shaving cream sit on your face for a while before you start. Don't be in a hurry. Shaving and speed don't mix. Never use a dull blade." He ran the razor under hot water.

Beekman watched every move. He hung on every word.

"It'll be a while before you start shaving, even with the big dance coming up," Leo continued. "I'll tell you right now to wait as long as you can before starting. But you won't. I didn't."

Leo made a long, slow stroke with the razor from a point just below his ear to his chin. "Shave down on your face and up on your neck," he said. "You can train your whiskers to grow that way. Saves a lot of skin pulling and cuts. Ow!" Leo nicked himself on the right side of his chin. "The most important thing to remember," he said, examining where he'd cut himself, "is to do as your old man says, not as he does."

Watching his father bleed, Beekman decided he'd put off shaving until the last possible moment.

"Unfortunately for you," Leo continued, "cutting yourself while shaving is in the genes. My old man used to come out of the bathroom in the morning with little pieces of toilet paper stuck to cuts all over his face."

Maybe he'd grow a beard, Beekman thought. "Where are you going on your date tonight?"

"Benny's," Leo said. "He still owes me nineteen dinners."

"Is it romantic?"

"What do you know about romantic?"

"Low lights. Soft music."

Leo laughed. "That's Benny's all right." He worked the razor up his neck.

"Pop?"

"What?"

"You should go out with Fernanda sometime."

"Think so?"

"Definitely."

"What makes you think she'd go out with me?"

"Why don't you ask her and find out?"

"Maybe I will."

"You definitely should."

"Okay, I definitely will."

"When?"

"Soon."

"How soon?"

"Is tonight soon enough for you?"

"You're taking Fernanda to Benny's tonight?"

"Eight o'clock reservation," Leo said.

"Excellent," Beekman said. The ship was launched.

# 15

## Another Peavy

"How about it, Beekman?" Marcus asked a hundred times on Monday. And a hundred times on Tuesday. And Wednesday. And Thursday. "How about coming home with me after school on Friday and having dinner and then we'll walk to the dance because Wembley Hall is only a couple of blocks from where I live. Then you'll sleep over afterwards. How about it, Beekman?"

Marcus asked Beekman to sleep over so many times that Beekman finally said yes. Anything to shut him up. Marcus Peavy was driving Beekman crazy. Otherwise, the week went about as well as Beekman could have expected; he got through his classes, Searle hit him only once, and he avoided the mighty McCann.

Even so, only Marcus's incredible persistence got Beekman off the bus at Eighty-sixth Street and Park Avenue on Friday afternoon.

"You can't change your mind now," Marcus said, his voice ringing with insistence. Beekman was holding tight to a pole by the open back door, looking out at the street like he was being asked to jump into an erupting volcano.

"Elizabeth is already cooking dinner," Marcus said. "Mother is expecting you. Elizabeth is making chocolate pie for dessert. She almost never makes chocolate pie."

Marcus grabbed Beekman's arm and pulled him to the sidewalk. "We're going to have fun," he said.

As they approached the old brick building, the doorman, whose name was Gustav, stepped out to greet them.

"Good afternoon, Marcus," Gustav said. He spoke with an eastern European accent.

Marcus introduced Beekman as his best friend.

Gustav bowed slightly from the waist and smiled at Beekman, revealing a gold tooth. "It's an honor to meet you," he said.

Beekman bowed back and told Gustav that the honor was his. He'd talk to Marcus about this best-friend business later.

"We live on the seventh floor," Marcus said as the elevator crept upward like it was making its way through goo. "There are eleven floors altogether. Four apartments on a floor. I've lived here all my life."

Marcus opened the door with his key and they entered a short hallway with a coat closet. "Come on," he said, leading Beekman to the kitchen. "I'll introduce you to Elizabeth."

"So you're the famous Beekman O'Day," Elizabeth said from behind the stove. She was tall and thin and her long gray hair was done up in a ponytail.

"And you're the famous Elizabeth," Beekman said back.

"I am indeed," she said, slipping them each an oatmeal raisin cookie.

Marcus led Beekman past the dining room and living room. "Elizabeth comes every afternoon," he said. "She shops and cooks and gets things ready. Mother gets home from work around five-thirty. Father comes later."

They passed a door with a large STAY OUT! sign taped to it. "That's my so-called sister's cave," Marcus said.

"I didn't know you had a sister," Beekman said.

"She's not something I like to talk about," Marcus said.

Beekman followed him into a room that was almost as small as his. A bunk bed was against one wall, a desk, computer, chair, and bookcase against another. Movie posters covered the walls.

"How old is she?" Beekman asked, dumping his backpack on the floor.

"Who?"

"Your sister."

"She's an hour older than me," Marcus said. "She came from a completely separate fertilized ova. We're dizygotic." Marcus saw Beekman's confusion. "We're fraternal twins. We don't look anything alike. We don't think anything alike. We're not alike in any way. She's from a different part of the universe. She goes to Wembley Hall."

"What does she look like?"

"Ugly," Marcus said. "Let's watch a movie. Choose whichever one you like. I've seen them all." He pointed to his bookcase. "I have westerns, detective stories, comedies, musicals, and what I call the classics. They're all old. One of my favorites is *Tom Brown's School Days*. The 1951 version."

"We can watch that one," Beekman said. He didn't

care. He was occupied with the prospect of this new Peavy.

"You think life at Chance is tough," Marcus said, leading the way to the living room and the TV, "wait until you see this."

Beekman stared at the STAY OUT! sign as they passed it. He wondered what she looked like and if she was as big a pain as her brother.

"We have to keep the sound down," Marcus said, "or Hydra will slither forth from her den and confiscate my movie and then I'll have to run an errand to get it back."

Beekman wondered about the power of this sister.

Mrs. Peavy came home at five-fifteen and introduced herself to Beekman. She seemed happy that Marcus had a friend. Mr. Peavy arrived at five forty-five. He was a large, lumbering man. Mrs. Peavy was petite. They gathered around the dining room table for an early dinner. Baked chicken and fried potatoes the size of carrots, baby peas and salad greens waited to be passed. One chair remained empty.

"Tell your sister I'm running out of patience," Mrs. Peavy said to her son.

"Do I have to?" Marcus complained. "She'll just yell at me and you know she won't come until she's ready anyway."

"I'll do it," Beekman said, trying not to sound too enthusiastic.

"Why not?" Mrs. Peavy said. "Go ahead."

"You'll be sorry," Marcus said.

"Good luck," Mr. Peavy said.

Beekman approached the STAY OUT! sign cautiously. He knocked lightly.

"Go away," the voice inside said. "I'm busy."

He knocked again.

"Marcus, don't make me come out there," the voice said.

"It's not Marcus," Beekman said. He realized that he didn't know her name. "Your mother said to tell you that everybody is waiting at the table." When he didn't get a response, he kept going. "Elizabeth made baked chicken and chocolate pie and I'm hungry and they won't eat without you."

The door opened six inches. Through the gap he saw a girl who was almost exactly his size. She had hair the color of new wheat. She had gray-green eyes and a small mouth and her nose had a small bump along its bridge, which he thought most appealing. She looked directly at him without blinking.

"Who are you?" she asked in a voice that was quiet, but tempered with steel.

"I'm Beekman O'Day," Beekman said, his heart rate accelerating rapidly.

"That's too bad," she said, marching past him. She was wearing a navy blue skirt that touched her knobby knees and a white blouse. The uniform of Wembley Hall.

"What's your name?" Beekman asked as he followed her to the dining room.

"Mary Louise," she said without looking back at him. "But I'd prefer it if you didn't call me anything. I'd prefer it if you didn't talk to me at all."

# 16

## The Dance

Beekman looked at himself in the mirror. All he'd brought with him for the dance was a clean shirt. How could he have known that he was going to meet Mary Louise? His pants and blazer were baggy from a week of wear. His hair had gone berserk. Even Marcus, in his dark brown suit, looked better than he did. This was not the impression he wanted to make. He heard voices outside Marcus's room. Two of Mary Louise's friends from Wembley Hall had come to walk with her to the dance. There was nothing he could do about his appearance but make the best of it.

"Let's walk with them," Beekman said, hurrying with the knot in his necktie.

"I'd rather walk barefoot through a cow pasture on a hot afternoon in August," Marcus said.

"We could follow right behind them," Beekman said.

"I'd rather sleep naked in Central Park in the middle of January," Marcus said.

Beekman heard Mary Louise and her friends saying goodbye to Mr. and Mrs. Peavy and hurried from the room. Marcus could do as he liked. He said his good-byes quickly. He just missed the elevator. It took forever for the second one to show up. When he reached the street Mary Louise and her friends were nowhere to be seen.

"What's your problem?" Marcus asked, emerging from the building behind him. "The dance doesn't start until seven-thirty and we absolutely do not want to get there early."

"What's your sister like to talk about?" Beekman asked. He'd use the time to prepare himself.

"How would I know?" Marcus said. "She never talks to me and I never talk to her. It's an arrangement we have."

"You must know something about her. She's your sister."

"Not only is she ugly," Marcus said, "she's also unpleasant. She's venomous. She exhales sulfuric acid."

"You're not being very helpful," Beekman said.

"I'm being honest."

"You don't like her because she's your sister."

"That's one reason," Marcus said. "There are a million more."

"You can't see her for what she really is," Beekman said.

"She's obnoxious. That's what she is."

"You must know something good about her."

"Let me think," Marcus said. "Nope. Not one thing. She is the most difficult human being I've ever met. Why are you asking me all these questions about her? She wouldn't give you the time of day if your life depended on it. She thinks you're an idiot. And worse than that, you're my friend. Which makes you a double idiot."

"Tell me about her anyway," Beekman said.

"Haven't you heard a word I've been saying? Wait a minute. I know what's going on here. You're going to ask her to dance."

"Of course I am," Beekman said.

"Why?" Marcus cried out. "Why would you subject yourself to torture if you don't have to?"

"You want me to be your friend, you'll help me with this," Beekman said.

"I don't know if I want to be your friend if you're going to like my sister," Marcus said.

They faced each other at the corner of Eighty-ninth Street and Madison Avenue. Wembley Hall was just down the block.

"The price of friendship runs high," Marcus said.

"Give me something I can work with," Beekman said. "Something that will impress her."

"She writes poetry," Marcus said.

"Poetry?"

"Verses. Couplets. Rhymes."

"I don't know anything about poetry," Beekman said.

"You must know one poem you can recite."

"I'll think of something. What else?"

"There is nothing else," Marcus said. "Just poetry. She spends all her time in her room reading it or writing it. She thinks she's Emily Dickinson."

"Who?"

"Emily Dickinson. The poet. She's dead, of course. My sister thinks all the great poets are dead. Except that she's going to become one someday. Just tell her you like Emily Dickinson."

They entered Wembley Hall's auditorium, which was decorated with piles of autumn leaves in baskets and bound-up bundles of cornstalks and pumpkins with painted faces. Mrs. Livermore, the mighty Mc-

Cann's counterpart, was onstage yelling into the microphone, which squeaked and squawked in protest.

"On behalf of the young women of the lower school of Wembley Hall," Mrs. Livermore yelled, "I welcome the young men of the lower school of Chance Academy. Welcome to our October dance."

Beekman spotted Mary Louise toward the back of the auditorium with her two friends. He offered her a smile when she caught him watching her. She frowned and he looked away.

"We have a few rules," Mrs. Livermore yelled into the microphone. "The first is that everybody dances. No wallflowers. Boys can ask girls, girls can ask boys, nobody can refuse. I don't want to see anybody standing around when the music is playing. There's no cutting in. Every dance is a complete dance. You can't dance more than one dance with the same partner." *Squeak-squawk, squeak-squawk,* went the sound system. It was like an enormous piece of bad chalk being pulled down a blackboard. "Space will be maintained between dancing partners at all times," she went on. "Mr. Keen and Miss Haymaker from Chance and Mr. Portnoy and Mrs. Beamis from Wembley Hall will see to it that the rules are adhered to."

Beekman looked around for Mary Louise and

couldn't find her, then did. She was hiding behind a tall gathering of cornstalks. He saw Searle approaching her general area, eyeing the girls like a hyena sizing up its crippled prey. He hoped that the mouth-breathing goon would leave Mary Louise alone. He hoped that Searle would stay clear of him. He didn't want any trouble. Not tonight.

The lights dimmed. A little. Not too much. Colored spotlights burst to life and bounced off the revolving mirrored ball that hung from the center of the ceiling. The walls became a kaleidoscope of red, yellow, blue, orange, and green dancing circles. The music began. A foxtrot. Beekman made a beeline for Mary Louise.

"May I have this dance?" he asked, standing on one side of the cornstalks while she remained on the other, looking off into the distance like he wasn't there. He was certain he sounded like an imbecile.

"I have to, don't I?" Mary Louise said, "now that you've asked me. I have no choice." She stepped out from behind the cornstalks. She was wearing a black skirt and red top and red socks and sandals, which Beekman knew were against the dress code. One more reason to admire her.

They moved cautiously to the dance floor and faced each other. "Let's get this over with," she said.

Beekman pictured the basic box step that Leo had

taught him the night before. It was all he knew of dancing. Forward together, side together, back together, side together.

"Let your feet go with the beat," Leo had said, "and you'll be all right."

Beekman and Leo had practiced for an hour. First Leo led, then Beekman. Until Beekman could do it with his eyes closed.

"Move with the music," Leo had said. "You'll be fine."

Beekman took a step forward and put a hand on Mary Louise's side. He held his other hand in the air in anticipation of receiving hers. He felt her hand on his side and her other hand taking his. He heard his father's voice in his ear. "Ask questions. Listen. Don't talk too much."

They began dancing. Much to Beekman's relief, she wasn't any better at it than he was.

"So we meet again," he said finally.

She looked at him like he was demented.

"You're a good dancer," he said.

"I stink," she said.

"So do I," he said.

"Yes, you do," she said.

Time to regroup. He looked around. He saw Marcus dancing with one of his sister's friends. Marcus rolled his eyes. Beekman gave him a thumbs-up. He was shoved from behind as Searle danced by. He wondered if garlic would keep Searle away.

"The decorations look good," Beekman said.

"They're feeble," Mary Louise said.

"How do you like Wembley Hall?" he countered.

"Do you work for a newspaper?" she asked.

"No," he said.

"Then why are you asking me all these questions?"

"I only asked you one question," Beekman said. "That's not exactly the third degree."

"I don't like people asking me questions," she said.

"I only brought it up because I've been to a lot of schools," he said.

She wasn't interested.

"The music is good," he ventured.

"It's dinky," she said.

"What classes are you taking this year?" he asked.

"Not very interesting ones," she said.

"You don't look anything like Marcus," he said.

"I got lucky," she said.

"Think the planet might get hit by an asteroid anytime soon?" he asked. He hoped the question would generate a smile. Nothing. This wasn't as easy as Leo had said it would be.

"If you'd rather not dance with me," Beekman said,

"I don't mind. We could stand in a corner and try to have a conversation."

"We have to dance the whole dance," she said. "It's one of the rules."

"I don't like rules," Beekman said.

She looked at him with a momentary spark of interest.

"Rules are meant to be broken," he continued, feeling a rush of confidence.

"Some are, some aren't," Mary Louise said. "And it's not something you talk about. It's something you do."

"Right," he said. She'd actually sounded civil. "Do you like poetry?" he asked. Time for the breakthrough.

She cocked her head to one side and her nose crinkled and her mouth worked its way into the slightest of smiles. "It depends," she said.

"Emily Dickinson," he said.

"What about her?"

"Emily Dickinson," he said again, trying to buy time. What could he say about Emily Dickinson?

"I heard you the first time," she said.

"She's dead," he said.

"Since 1886," she said.

"She was a poet," he said. This was going better than he'd expected.

"The best American poet who ever lived," she said. "Do you know any of her poems?"

He felt his head going up and down in the affirmative. What was he doing? What was he going to say?

" 'It's such a little thing to weep,' " Mary Louise recited, " 'So short a thing to sigh; / And yet by trades the size of these / We men and women die!' "

"That's a great poem," Beekman said. He was off the hook. "Do another one."

"Your turn," she said.

"Roses are red," he said, without giving it a nanosecond's worth of thought, "violets are blue. / I know I like dancing because I'm dancing with you." It wasn't Emily Dickinson, but he thought maybe she'd like it anyway.

"You don't know anything about poetry," she said.

"It rhymed," he said.

"You don't know anything about Emily Dickinson. Marcus put you up to this. He's a drip and so are you."

"I was just trying to have a conversation," Beekman said. "I don't know why you're getting so upset." The music stopped. "You could be a nicer person. You could do something about that." He watched her walk away, convinced that he'd spent the last four minutes dancing on his tongue.

After that he moved around a lot and danced as lit-

**118**

tle as possible. He watched, even though he didn't want to, Mary Louise dance with Foyle, Wibble, Carnaby, Samuels, Mingus, and the rest of his class and half of the second form. Then he saw Searle swaggering across the auditorium as a new song began. He saw Searle saying something to Mary Louise. He saw Searle putting his apelike arms around her. He saw her struggling to pull away. He charged across the floor.

"Leave her alone!" Beekman yelled. He saw Searle turn and smile, like he'd planned it this way. Mary Louise looked horrified. "Let her go," he commanded. He pulled at Searle's arm. Searle shook him off like a fly. Mary Louise yanked herself free from Searle's clutches.

"I don't need you to do my fighting for me," she said to Beekman.

"Beek the freak couldn't fight an old lady," Searle said, delivering a short, hard uppercut to Beekman's midsection that nobody, including Mary Louise, who was standing right there, noticed.

Except Beekman himself, who grunted as quietly as he could. *"Umpfff,"* he said, sounding like a tire leaking air. He plastered a smile on his face. He wasn't going to let her see him in pain.

"Leave me alone," Mary Louise said to Beekman.

"Go back under the rock where you live," she said to Searle.

"We haven't finished our dance," Searle said, taking hold of her.

"You're a swine," she said, trying to pull away.

Beekman grabbed Searle's jacket and pulled as hard as he could. "I'm going to knock your head off," he yelled. "I'm going to mop up the floor with you." He saw Searle making a fist. He felt a hand slap down hard on his shoulder.

"What's going on here?" Miss Haymaker asked, inserting herself between Beekman and Searle.

"Nothing," Mary Louise said, walking away.

"Beek the freak is making trouble again," Searle said, going off in another direction. "He's always making trouble."

Miss Haymaker turned her attention to Beekman. "What do you have to say for yourself?" she asked.

"Would you like to dance?" he responded.

"Chaperones aren't allowed to dance," Miss Haymaker said. "Otherwise, I'd be delighted. Stay away from Searle. Stay out of trouble."

"I will," Beekman said. "You can count on it." When Miss Haymaker continued on her rounds, he headed straight for Mary Louise.

"I can take care of myself," she said when she saw him.

"Searle's a moron," Beekman said. "You can't let him bother you. If brains were dynamite, he wouldn't have enough power in there to blow his nose."

"That's an attractive picture," she said. "Thank you."

"Just trying to cheer you up."

"You can do that by going away."

"Sure," he said. "I'm wasting my time talking to you anyway." He tried to walk off casually, as though it didn't matter one way or the other whether she liked him or not. He'd be cool. Maybe that would work. He looked back. She wasn't even watching him.

# 17

## The Old Leather Suitcase

Mary Louise did not show up for breakfast. Beekman was thunderstruck with disappointment. He'd spent half the night in Marcus's lower bunk planning what he was going to say.

"Don't you care what she does in there?" Marcus complained to his mother and father at the table.

"I'm happier not knowing," Mrs. Peavy said.

"I think you should make her get up," Marcus said. "I think you should make her eat breakfast with us."

"Breakfast is the most important meal of the day," Beekman said. How could she not show up? He had to leave soon.

"It's the weekend," Mr. Peavy said. "Let her sleep."

"She gets whatever she wants," Marcus said, then let it drop.

When he could wait no longer, Beekman thanked Marcus's parents for their hospitality, told Marcus he'd be delighted to stay over anytime, then ran as fast as he could to catch the bus. He had Saturday school.

There were three of them in Mr. Jack's classroom. Beekman didn't know the other two. They were from the upper school. They ignored him. Mr. Jack made the same speech he made every Saturday morning.

"I'm Mr. Jack," Mr. Jack said. "Thirty years ago I was hired to teach *government studies*, not run a Saturday nursery school for misfits." Beekman knew for a fact that Mr. Jack had been doing this as long as he'd been doing everything else at Chance. "Anybody caught *not* studying," Mr. Jack continued, "will get an *extra* Saturday." Then he excused himself with the warning that he'd be back unexpectedly.

Beekman left the room as soon as Mr. Jack was gone. He ran down the stairs and into the library. He found the biography section. By the time Mr. Jack returned to his classroom, Beekman was bent over his desk reading, preparing himself for the day when he would discuss Emily Dickinson with Mary Louise and prove his interest in what mattered to her most.

That afternoon, Beekman and his father sweated through a workout.

"How was the dance?" Leo asked.

"Good," Beekman said.

"Did you meet anybody you liked?"

"I did."

"What's her name?"

"Mary Louise," Beekman said. "She's Marcus Peavy's twin sister, except she's way better-looking. She goes to Wembley Hall. I danced with her."

"You going to see her again?"

"Definitely," Beekman said.

They finished working their arms and moved on to their legs. After that would come the treadmill and then the abs. Crunch time.

"I have to go out tonight," Leo said when they were getting dressed. "I've got a deal cooking. Shouldn't be gone more than a couple of hours."

"I'm doing my homework tonight," Beekman said. Failing his classes was not going to impress Mary Louise. "What's the deal?"

"This guy in New Jersey owns a fleet of used rental cars and he's looking to trade them for an industrial building in Yonkers. It's a nice commission."

"Knock 'em dead, Pop," Beekman said.

When Leo left for New Jersey, Beekman set himself up at his desk. He opened his Latin book, determined to get through an entire chapter before he closed it. Soon he was staring out his window.

He saw Moxie LaMoca in a tuxedo heading for work. A few minutes later, he saw Sergio West pass by in the other direction with a bag of groceries. Fernanda's lights weren't on yet. She hadn't returned from wherever she was. A policeman knocked at Madam de Campo's door. He came once a week to have his fortune told.

Beekman opened his math book, then closed it. He couldn't concentrate on numbers. History would require less brainpower. The dates danced on the page. He picked up the book on Emily Dickinson and started looking for a poem to memorize.

When he focused again, he found himself staring through the open door of his closet at the entrance to the storage area. The old leather suitcase that his father had hauled with him every time they'd moved was on the other side of that wall. Beekman knew what was inside it. At least he was pretty sure he knew. It was time to find out if he was right. He went downstairs and got the flashlight, then made his way into the storage area on his hands and knees. He found it in a corner, beneath some boxes, and pulled it out. It was light. Too light maybe to be holding anything at all.

He set the suitcase on the floor of his room and examined it. The leather was badly cracked. The combination lock was corroded. He tried to turn the little wheels. They were stuck. He had no idea what the combination was anyway. He went downstairs to the kitchen junk drawer and got a screwdriver. He used it to break the lock. He opened the suitcase.

A layer of tissue paper greeted him. He removed it carefully. He found more tissue paper, which was wrapped around a thick rectangle of fabric. He unfolded a large scarf of many colors. He put it to his face and inhaled and discovered the long-ago fragrance of his mother.

He put the scarf aside and turned his attention to the large envelope that came next. In it were his mother and father's marriage certificate, his birth certificate, and his mother's death certificate. He studied the first two, then tried to read the death certificate, but the words kept blurring, so he put it down.

Next came a layer of photographs in clear plastic sleeves. The date and place were written on the back of each one in a hand he'd never seen before. It had to be his mother's writing. It was the first time he'd ever seen it. He lingered over each picture. There was one of his mother as a young girl of maybe twelve or thirteen. He could see himself in her thin, bony frame and in the earnestness of her expression. There was one of her and Leo at an amusement park eating ice cream. She couldn't have been more than twenty. In their wedding picture, his mother held a small bunch of white flowers. She and Leo were looking at each other like they were the only two people in the world. There was a photograph of his mother and Leo at the beach looking tanned and happy. His mother smiled in all of them, but not nearly so much as in the last, when she was so obviously pregnant with him. He looked through them a second time. His mother had been beautiful, he thought. She'd been happy.

Beekman opened the small box that came next. He found his mother's wedding ring—a plain simple band of gold—a thin necklace with a locket attached to it, a bracelet of small colored stones with little figures of beetles carved in them, and her wristwatch. The watch had stopped at 4:22. He wondered if it had stopped in the morning or afternoon. He wondered if she'd been wearing it. He clutched the wedding ring tightly in his hand. He felt his mother's warmth. The locket had a photograph of Leo in it.

He wondered about the sound of his mother's voice

and what it would be like to hear her call his name. He wondered what it would be like to have her ask him about his day at school. And what it would be like to have the three of them at the table eating dinner together. To have her here so he could tell her about Mary Louise Peavy and ask her advice.

He picked up the death certificate, determined this time to get through it. He saw his mother's name and the name of the hospital and the name of a doctor. He saw that the cause of her death was heart failure. His eye caught the date of her death. It was the date of his birth.

His mother had died the day he was born. He was responsible for his mother's death. What other conclusion could he come to? How his mother died was a secret his father had kept from him. Now he had to live with it. He had killed his own mother.

# 18

## His Mother's Things

When Leo came home from New Jersey, Beekman was waiting up for him.

"It's eleven-thirty," Leo said. "You should be in bed."

Beekman didn't say anything.

"You okay?" Leo hung his coat in the closet.

Beekman shrugged his shoulders.

"The building deal didn't work out," Leo said. He went to the refrigerator to get a beer. "The guy with the building wanted more cars. The guy with the cars wanted more building. Something bigger. Sometimes you can't make anybody happy."

"I know why you won't talk about my mother," Beekman said.

"I talk about her," Leo said.

"No, you don't," Beekman said, his raspy voice growing raspier.

His father gave him a sharp look.

"You always change the subject," Beekman said.

"We can talk about her in the morning," Leo said.

"You always put it off."

"I'm tired," Leo said.

"I want to talk about her now."

"It's been a long day," Leo said. He headed for his bedroom.

"I don't want to wait anymore," Beekman said. "I want to talk about her tonight. Before I go to bed. I want you to tell me about her."

"In the morning," Leo snapped.

"Now!" Beekman snapped back.

"No!" Leo said. "Not now."

Beekman could tell how hard his father was working to hold on to his temper.

"We'll talk tomorrow," Leo said. "When we're both feeling better." He closed the door of his bedroom behind him.

"I opened the suitcase," Beekman yelled. "I broke the lock and I looked at what was in it."

"That suitcase is none of your business," Leo yelled

as he yanked open the door. "You had no right to look in it."

"Why didn't you tell me she died when I was born?" Beekman yelled. "I killed her, didn't I?"

"What are you talking about?" Leo asked. "Where did you get that idea?"

"It says so on the death certificate," Beekman said. "It says she died on the same day I was born. I saw it. I killed her."

"You didn't kill her," Leo said. He moved to take his son in his arms. "You had nothing to do with her dying."

"I'll show you," Beekman said, breaking free of his father's clumsy embrace. He ran up the stairs, Leo close behind him.

"You didn't kill her," Leo said. "It had nothing to do with you." He ducked to get into his son's room.

"It says so right here," Beekman said. He held up the death certificate. "It says she died when I was born."

"She died hours after you were born," Leo said. "The two things had nothing to do with each other." He took the death certificate from Beekman. His hand trembled. When he spoke again, Beekman could barely hear him. "The wall of her heart gave way," Leo said. "It was weak in one tiny spot. So tiny nobody knew anything was wrong. Not her. Not me. Not the doctors. It just happened. Nobody killed her. You can't think like that. I won't let you." He grabbed his son and this time held on to him. "It wasn't you," he said. "It wasn't you."

"Then why do you always act like there's some kind of secret when I want to talk about her?" Beekman asked. "Why don't we have pictures of her? Why don't I have something that belonged to her?"

"You have her name," Leo said. He looked around the room as though he were searching for something.

Beekman could see the pain gathering in his father's face. "Why didn't you ever show me what was in the suitcase?" he asked.

"I wasn't there," Leo said finally. "I wasn't with her. I was in Cleveland. Making a deal. I thought I'd be back in time. I called the hospital and they said I had a healthy son and that my wife was doing fine. I was going to forget about the deal and come back then, but I stayed. Just for another hour or two, I thought. Until they signed. Her heart stopped while I was getting on the plane. I should have been with her when you were born. I should have been with her when she died."

Beekman saw the tears in his father's eyes. He felt his own eyes flooding.

"Do you want to look through her things together?" Leo asked.

Beekman nodded. They sat on the floor by the suitcase.

Leo started with the photographs.

# 19

## In His Father's Footsteps

They stood in front of the mirror singing "Bye Bye Blackbird," doing a little dance to go with it. Leo was wearing his gray pinstriped suit and Beekman was in freshly pressed gray flannels and his blue blazer. As they reached the last couple of lines, they split into harmony. Beekman took the high road and Leo the low, and by the time they arrived at the end, they achieved a near perfect blend of voices. They bowed to the mirror, then to each other.

But Beekman's heart wasn't in it this morning. After looking through his mother's things with his father, Leo had told him that he was glad to have the suitcase open. That it felt good to talk. He told Beekman how he and his mother had met and what her favorite foods were and her favorite color and her favorite music, and he'd tried to explain what she'd sounded like.

"She was from Queens," Leo had said. "She had a New York accent you could hear a mile away. She sounded like an angel."

Beekman had seen how much his father missed his mother. Listening to him talk about her, Beekman had never felt closer to Leo. He'd accepted Leo's version of events. He'd decided to believe that he hadn't killed his mother after all.

That's when he discovered he had a new problem. In thinking about all that Leo had told him about his mother, he realized how little he knew about his father. He'd lived his whole life with Leo. He had no idea really what his father did for a living. Making deals wasn't a business. Why didn't his father have a regular job, like Mr. Peavy or Loomis Garcia? They went to work every day and got a paycheck. They knew what was what with the rent and the rest of their lives.

"I have a hot one in the fire," Leo said, adjusting his necktie.

"Why can't you put the cars-and-building deal back together?" Beekman asked.

"Deals are a lot like Humpty Dumpty," Leo said. "This one was shaky from the start."

"How come so many deals don't happen?" Beekman asked.

"Everything has to be just right for a deal to go through," Leo said. "The people involved, what they have and what they want, the timing, you have to have all that, then the stars have to be in alignment and the moon has to be full. Something, anything, the smallest thing falls out of place and the deal is kaput. Finis. That's what happens most of the time. The new one I'm working on has *winner* written all over it. Fur-covered musical toilet seats."

Beekman snorted a laugh of disbelief.

"Go ahead and laugh," Leo said, reshaping his handkerchief into the breast pocket of his jacket. "But there they are. A warehouse full of fur-covered musical toilet seats. They play songs when you sit down. 'Twinkle, Twinkle Little Star.' 'Row, Row, Row Your Boat.' The theme from *The Godfather*. And they keep your bottom warm. What more could you ask?"

"I can't think of a thing," Beekman said.

"They made too many of them," Leo said, "which isn't difficult to understand. I've got a one-week exclusive. I'm talking to somebody I know in Alaska."

"Alaska sounds like the place for fur-covered musical toilet seats," Beekman said. He wondered how long it would take to go crazy from hearing the same song over and over again.

They sang and danced another chorus of "Bye Bye Blackbird."

"We should be on the stage," Leo said when they were done.

"There's one leaving in five minutes," Beekman said.

"That's an old joke," Leo said.

"The good jokes never get old," Beekman said.

They left together, encountering Madam de Campo as they stepped outside. She was wearing a purple cape and purple earmuffs and a wide-brimmed purple hat with a large artificial purple flower sticking up from its crown.

"It's the Mr. O'Days," Madam de Campo said. She looked at Beekman as though receiving some kind of message that was coming through the air. "It's a great day for an adventure," Madam de Campo said to him. Then she leaned forward and whispered in his ear, "Knock on my door when you're ready to have your future looked into. I'll be waiting." Whistling, she bustled off.

Beekman and Leo walked to the corner. "As of this morning," Leo said, "we're down to our last couple of servings of groats. I can get us another hundred-pound bag if you're interested."

"I'd prefer old rubber tires," Beekman said.

"I can get us a deal on those too," Leo said. "Re-treads taste the best."

"How about pancakes?" Beekman asked. "Would pancakes possibly be okay?"

"I'll see what I can do," Leo said.

They inhaled deeply of the early November air. There was a taste of winter in it.

"A new week filled with new possibilities," Leo said. "A big day ahead."

Beekman watched his father walk off, looking as he always did, like he owned the world. A bus slowed as it approached the stop and Beekman ran to catch it. He started to get on, then looked back. He could still see Leo. He let the bus go without him. So what if he missed a day of school. All the mighty McCann would do was add more Saturday sessions to the ones he already had. His decision was an impulse born of concern.

Where did his father go every day? He knew Leo had an office, but its whereabouts changed so often he wasn't always sure where it was. Or even if it really existed. And why did Leo have a lot of money sometimes and hardly any the rest of the time? Maybe what his father did was illegal. Maybe Leo was some sort of criminal. If his father could keep secrets about his mother all these years, maybe there were other secrets as well.

It was easy to keep Leo in sight. Beekman got within half a block of him, then maintained that distance. On Twenty-eighth Street, Leo stopped at a flower stall. Beekman ducked into a doorway and saw his father emerge a few minutes later with a yellow flower wrapped in green paper. He followed Leo downtown, then over to Broadway, where his father entered a coffee shop.

Beekman took a deep breath, then inched forward and peeked in through the coffee shop's window. He exhaled his relief. Leo was sitting with his back to the street. Across the table from him sat a man with a briefcase on his lap. Beekman wondered if he should go inside. He wondered if he could get close enough to listen and still be safe. Then he thought, if he did what was safe, he'd never find out anything.

He went inside and made his way along the counter to a stool that put him right behind his father. Leo wouldn't see him unless he turned all the way around. For good measure, Beekman imagined himself invisible.

"What'll you have?" the waiter behind the counter shouted at Beekman.

"Small orange juice," Beekman mumbled.

"What?" the waiter shouted.

"Small orange juice," Beekman said, trying to disguise his voice.

"Small orange juice," the waiter shouted. "That it?"

"Yes," Beekman said between his teeth.

The waiter wrote out Beekman's check and slapped it down in front of him. "One small orange juice coming up," he shouted as he walked away.

Beekman turned until he could just see the back of his father's head from the corner of his eye. He tuned in.

"Two hundred and fifty laptops," the man across from Leo said. "All new. Major manufacturer. The boxes have never been opened."

"What do you want for them?" Leo asked.

"I'm in the distribution business," the man said. "I supply street vendors with merchandise. Watches. CD players. Sunglasses. Umbrellas. Along those lines. I need something that won't call attention to itself on the street."

"Where'd you get the laptops?" Leo asked.

"You don't need to know that," the man said.

"You want to trade something that was stolen for something you can sell on the street," Leo said. "Not my line of work."

"You were recommended," the man said.

"Somebody made a mistake," Leo said, standing. He put money on the table. "That's for my coffee."

Beekman turned away and shielded his face with his hand.

"Here's your orange juice, kid," the waiter shouted as he set it on the counter.

Leo brushed against Beekman as he left.

Beekman held his breath.

"Excuse me," Leo said without looking.

# 20

## O'Day Enterprises

Beekman followed his father down Broadway. He hid in a doorway when Leo stopped to look at the display in a bookstore window. He hid again when Leo went into a deli to buy a lottery ticket. He followed Leo across Union Square, through the outdoor farmers' market. He watched Leo buy an apple, then followed him to a small office building. He saw Leo get on the elevator and disappear. He waited a moment, then went inside and checked the directory. O'Day Enterprises was on the ninth floor.

The elevator returned. Beekman stepped aboard. An old woman with curly red hair that looked like a hat stood ramrod straight at the controls. Her uniform was maroon.

"Step to the rear of the car," she ordered, even though there was nobody else getting on. She turned to look at Beekman. "What floor?"

"Nine, please," Beekman said. He saw a yellow flower pinned to her shirt. "That's a nice flower," he said.

"A gift from an admirer," she said. She lowered her button of a nose to sniff it, then reached out and closed the door.

It was a slow ride. The old lady elevator operator hummed the whole way. She made a perfect landing at the ninth floor.

"Thank you," Beekman said as he stepped out.

She winked, closed the door, and was gone.

Beekman looked up and down the corridor. It was lined with doors to small, individual offices. He made his way past room numbers 900 and 901 and 902, and past eleven more, until he approached O'Day Enterprises, which was located in room 914, the last one on the left. The door was closed. The light was on inside. Beekman could see it through the open transom. If he had something to stand on, he might be able to hear what was going on on the other side. But there was nothing to stand on and the mail slot in the door had a guard over it.

He saw that there was no light on in the office next to Leo's. That transom was open too. The door gave way to a turn of the knob and a gentle push. Except for a dented metal wastebasket, the room was empty. Beekman closed the door, set his backpack down, turned the wastebasket over, sat on it, and pressed his ear to the wall that connected him to his father's office. He heard Leo's chair squeal on its wheels. He heard the phone ring.

"Leo O'Day Enterprises," he heard his father say.

Then, with pauses in between, Beekman heard: "Olive oil? How many gallons? Is it the first pressing? Where did it come from? What do you want for it? I'll get back to you."

A minute later he heard his father's voice again. He heard the olive oil being traded for a thousand movie tickets. Another call was made. He heard his father saying that the deal was done.

"If it's all the same to you," he heard his father say, "I'll take the cash. No movie tickets. No olive oil. Cash. It's worth at least thirty-five hundred."

Beekman heard his father accept twelve hundred and fifty.

He heard his father make a series of calls to drum

up business. These must have been to old customers, Beekman thought, because the conversations were brief and Leo called people by their first names.

Then Beekman heard the phone ring again. He heard his father's greeting. He heard the name Mr. Rumble. Mr. Rumble was the bursar at Chance Academy.

"I know I'm late," Beekman heard his father say. "I told you I'd get it in and I will. Nothing is more important to me than Beekman staying at Chance. I'll make sure you get your money. Next week at the latest. You've got a great school and we're proud to be part of it. Next week for sure. I'll bring it up myself. Thank you for your patience, Mr. Rumble."

Beekman couldn't believe it. His father hadn't paid Chance. He'd been there less than two months and already they were behind. He wasn't going to last until Christmas. He heard Leo close the door to his office and head down the corridor. He grabbed his backpack and ran to the stairs and raced down them and out through the lobby to the street and just caught sight of Leo turning the corner and heading west.

It was lunchtime and the streets were packed tight. Now it wasn't easy to keep Leo in sight. He nearly lost him twice. Leo went into a restaurant, the kind that requires a reservation. All Beekman could do was wait outside.

He saw a hot dog cart across the street. Standing next to it, keeping an eye on the restaurant while he ate his hot dog, Beekman felt like a cop on undercover duty. He felt bad about spying on his father, but he had to know.

After lunch, Leo went back to his office and Beekman spent the afternoon listening to his father make cold calls, trying to sell his services. The pitch was pretty much always the same.

"I can trade your excess inventory, or I can find something you're looking for and arrange a trade for that. I can find anything. I can trade anything. I've been doing it for twenty years. I work on a cash commission. The fee is negotiable."

Beekman had heard enough. He left the building and walked home. That his father didn't rob banks for a living was a matter of great relief. But the deals were all little deals. Olive oil and movie tickets. There were no big deals. Leo had made them all up. And business stunk anyway. They weren't making any money and he'd have to leave Chance and they'd have to move again.

Marcus Peavy was waiting for him at Nutting Court. "Where were you today?" he demanded.

"Busy," Beekman said. He unlocked the door and went inside.

"Are you sick?" Marcus said, entering behind him. "Is that why you missed school?"

"It doesn't concern you," Beekman said.

"I have your homework assignments," Marcus said. "We have a Latin test tomorrow. I came to make sure you were all right."

"I'm all right," Beekman said. "You can go home now."

Marcus headed for the kitchen. "Do you have anything to eat?" he asked. He opened the refrigerator and peered in. "I met Madam de Campo while I was waiting for you," Marcus said. "She said, and I quote, 'Beekman O'Day is lucky to have you for a friend.' Also, Sergio West stopped to look me over like I was some sort of criminal until I explained who I was. He knew all about Chance. They both knew that you'd missed school. I wouldn't mind a cheese sandwich."

Beekman made them cheese on wheat bread with mustard and mayonnaise. He'd do his homework. Why not? It would take his mind off his father and their situation. And it was the only way he could get rid of Marcus Peavy.

# 21

## Beekman's Chance

"What are you going to tell the mighty McCann?" Marcus asked Beekman as they opened their Latin books.

Beekman shrugged his shoulders. It wasn't something he wanted to think about. He didn't want to think about anything.

"You're in big trouble without an excuse," Marcus said. "You're going to have to come up with something really good."

"I've been in trouble before," Beekman said.

"Not with somebody like the mighty McCann. He never gives anybody a break. Will your father write you a note? That would do it."

"He doesn't know I missed school."

"He's going to find out."

"I'll worry about it then."

"Sooner or later you're going to tell me what you did today," Marcus said. "Save yourself the trouble and tell me now."

Beekman gave Marcus a hard look.

"I could say I came here after school and found you sick in bed," Marcus said.

"My father and I left the house together."

"You could say you got sick on the way to school and had to come back."

"Maybe," Beekman said, to get Marcus to stop. He knew he wasn't going to stay at Chance no matter what he said.

"I'll wait until your father comes home," Marcus said. "I'll tell him you got sick on the way to school and I came to see how you were. Then he can tell the mighty McCann."

Leo showed up shortly thereafter. Beekman introduced him to Marcus.

"It's a great honor to meet the father of my best friend," Marcus said.

"Stay for dinner," Leo said to Marcus as he set the shopping bag of Chinese takeout on the counter. "I have enough food here for ten people."

"I have to go," Marcus said. "I'm only here because Beekman . . ."

"Because I needed help with my homework," Beekman said, cutting Marcus off at the pass. "He was just leaving." Beekman pushed Marcus out the door.

"What's wrong with you?" Marcus asked, annoyed. "You were supposed to be sick."

"I changed my mind."

"That was a good plan."

"I'll have a better plan tomorrow," Beekman said.

While they were chewing their way through egg rolls, chicken in black bean sauce, and green beans with peanuts, Leo talked about his prospects for the coming holiday season. Beekman thought about how hard his father had to work and how sad it was that making money was so much trouble.

"Things are definitely looking up," Leo said.

"The next phone call could be the big one," Beekman said, trying to sound encouraging.

"Who knows what tomorrow will bring," Leo said.

"I could help you," Beekman said. "We could work on deals together. I'll bet I'm good at it."

"Your deal is school," Leo said. "My deal is deals. When you're finished with school we can talk about working together."

"School is stupid," Beekman said.

"School is how you make something of yourself in this life," Leo said. "Being left out is no fun."

"I don't need school."

"You don't have that much left to go," Leo said. "Eighth grade next year. High school and college after that."

"That's nine years," Beekman said.

"It'll be over before you know it," Leo said. "Tell you what. Why don't we close out the year winners. You bring home a big report card, I'll close a big deal. Then we'll have something to celebrate."

That night Beekman thought about how complicated life was. Just when he thought he had a problem solved, another one came along to take its place. He fell asleep thinking there was no escape.

When he entered the mighty McCann's office after chapel the next morning, he had no idea what he was going to say.

"Where were you yesterday, Mr. O'Day?" the mighty McCann asked, getting directly to the point.

"I had to take the day off," Beekman said.

"And why was that?" the mighty McCann asked when Beekman offered nothing more.

"I can't say," Beekman said.

"Are you in some sort of difficulty?"

"No, sir," Beekman said. "Except with you."

"You have no explanation for your absence?"

"I needed a day off," Beekman said.

"I had high hopes for you, Mr. O'Day," the mighty McCann said. "You missed the last student council meeting. Do you have an excuse for that?"

Beekman didn't say anything. He'd forgotten all about it.

"I'm removing you from the student council," the mighty McCann said.

Beekman felt a twinge of regret. He didn't know why. Who cared about the student council?

"You don't think much of Chance Academy, do you?" the mighty McCann said.

Beekman started to say that he didn't like a single thing about it, but the words got stuck somewhere inside him.

"Perhaps you'd be happier at some other school," the mighty McCann said.

Beekman's "No!" croaked its way to the surface.

The mighty McCann looked at him, startled by the passion of Beekman's response.

Beekman was startled by it himself. "I want to stay here," he said. What was he doing? Why was he allowing himself to care about something he couldn't have? "I like it here. I didn't when I started, but I do now. I want to stay." He could barely believe it, but there it was.

"I'm putting you on probation, Mr. O'Day," the mighty McCann said. "For the rest of the semester. If you violate one more rule, if I have to call you into my office for any reason, you'll be expelled. Your future here is entirely in your hands."

Leo was chopping onions for spaghetti sauce when Beekman walked in. "Headmaster McCann called," Leo said. "Why did you miss school yesterday, son of mine?"

"I took a day off," Beekman said. "Everybody needs a day off once in a while."

"That's true," Leo said. "What did you do with your day off?"

"Personal stuff," Beekman said. He headed for the stairs. "I don't want to talk about it now."

"Now is when we're going to talk about it," Leo said. "Probation is serious. So is nobody knowing where you are."

Beekman stopped at the bottom of the stairs. He wanted to tell his father that he'd spied on him. That he knew what was going on. That there weren't any big deals, only little ones. That soon they'd be gone from Nutting Court and Chance would be a memory. But how could he tell him? What good would it do?

"I'll do better," Beekman said. "I promise."

"I don't want you to do better," Leo said. "I want you to do your best. You didn't break the law, did you?"

"No," Beekman said.

"The police aren't after you?"

"No."

"You're okay?"

"Yes."

"Do you need any help with anything?"

"No."

"You're sure?"

"I'm sure," Beekman said.

"No more days off without talking to me first," Leo said. "Agreed?"

"Agreed," Beekman said.

"No more trouble at school," Leo said. "That's part of the deal."

"No more trouble," Beekman said.

"Then you don't have to tell me," Leo said. "Probation is enough punishment. Go hit the books. Dinner in an hour."

Beekman headed up the stairs to his room. He

knew Leo was angry at him. He was angry too. About finding people he liked and having to leave them. About having to leave the only school where he felt he belonged. About being told to believe in a future that didn't exist.

# 22

## Losing It

He opened his Spanish book to study for a quiz, then got lost in thought about his mother and father and his life. About how confusing everything seemed. About how little he had to do with how things turned out. He tried Latin. He'd failed yesterday's test and had to take another in a week. He spent the ride uptown looking out the window. He changed to the crosstown bus. Marcus got on at Park Avenue.

"I've decided to wait for you in the morning," Marcus announced as he sat down next to Beekman. "That way I can help you with your work."

"How's your sister?" Beekman asked.

"She has a cold," Marcus said, getting out his Spanish book.

"So she's home in bed," Beekman said, thinking that this might be the perfect opportunity to bring her flowers. If he couldn't get anything else in his life to work right, he would make something of his relationship with Mary Louise.

"Are you kidding?" Marcus said. "My sister wouldn't miss school if she was dying. They'd have to lock her out. She takes advanced everything and never gets less than a hundred percent in any of it. She's never missed a day of school in her life. Not even when she had her broken leg."

"She broke her leg?" Beekman asked, his voice rasping with concern.

"It happened three years ago," Marcus said, looking at Beekman like he was beyond redemption. "Skiing. We went once. It was my father's idea. Part of his scheme to get us involved with the great outdoors. She broke it on the bunny slope. When the vacation was over, she was back in school, cast, crutches, and all. She's not human. The only thing that changes when she gets sick is that she becomes even meaner. You wouldn't think that was possible. You can get an upset stomach just by looking at her when she's sick."

Flowers were out. He'd have to think of something else. He'd do it today. While she wasn't feeling well. So she could see how much he cared.

As the bus made its way to the West Side, Marcus tried to help Beekman get ready for the quiz. He peppered him with questions. Beekman's thoughts had returned to his father. He wasn't sure what he could believe anymore.

At chapel, the mighty McCann spoke on the subject of personal responsibility. Beekman was convinced that he was the sole object of the lecture. On the way out, Searle thrust his elbow into Beekman's side.

"I'm going to do that to you all day," Searle hissed in Beekman's ear. "I'm going to make you black-and-blue all over."

"Why don't you leave me alone?" Beekman asked. "Go pick on somebody else."

"I'm going to make you sorry you came to this school," Searle said.

"Why?" Beekman asked. "I never did anything to you."

"I don't like you," Searle said.

"Maybe we could settle this some other way," Beekman said. "Maybe we could talk about it. Figure something out."

"I'm going to do what I'm going to do," Searle said,

"and you're not going to say anything about it because I'll say you started it and you'll get expelled because you're already on probation." Searle gave Beekman another shot in the ribs and walked off.

Beekman tried to concentrate on his classes. He tried to picture Mary Louise smiling at him. He conjured up a big deal for his father. But as the day wore on, it became increasingly difficult to do anything but anticipate what Searle was going to do next.

Searle was there after every class. Grinning. Grabbing. Holding on to Beekman with one hand while he administered short, hard punches to his sides and stomach with the other. Once he kicked Beekman in the shin, then stomped on his foot. In the lunchroom, Searle sat next to Beekman and pinched his legs beneath the table, squeezing the skin between his fingers until Beekman fled, his food untouched.

"What's going on with you and Searle?" Marcus asked, running after Beekman. Marcus hadn't caught Searle in the act, but he knew something was happening. He'd been waiting for Beekman to tell him.

"Nothing's going on," Beekman said.

"I'll help you," Marcus said.

"No," Beekman said.

"I know he's doing something to you," Marcus said.

"Leave me alone," Beekman said. He'd suffer Searle

as long as he could. He wasn't getting anyone else involved.

In between history and English, Beekman had to go to the bathroom. He couldn't put it off any longer. He snuck to the third floor and closed himself in a stall and raised his feet off the floor. When he emerged, Searle was leaning against a sink, his arms folded across his chest.

"Here's what we're going to do," Beekman said as soon as he saw him.

"What are we going to do?" Searle asked, momentarily confused.

"You're going to tell me why you're hitting me, then we're going to figure out how you can stop."

"I don't want to stop," Searle said. He unfolded his long arms and started cracking his knuckles.

"If we could find out what the reason is," Beekman said, "we could do something about it."

"The reason is I like it," Searle said. "It makes me feel better."

"Hitting people shouldn't make you feel better," Beekman said.

"But it does," Searle said.

Enough is enough, Beekman thought. He was dealing with somebody whose brain was the size of a bean. A very small bean. Nothing he could say was going to make any difference. He went to a sink to wash his hands. "Why don't you go check yourself into a home for the deranged," he said.

"Why don't you go downstairs and tell McCann you're quitting," Searle said.

"I wouldn't quit anything because of you," Beekman said.

"You will when I'm done," Searle said, moving toward Beekman, his fist rising in the air.

An upper-school teacher walked in.

After history, Searle pushed Beekman down the stairs. It was just a shove and it wasn't all the way down, just the first half dozen steps.

Searle hurried down the stairs after him. "Let me help you," he said loud enough for anybody nearby to hear. He offered his hand.

Beekman kept his eye on Searle's other hand, the one he knew would strike out at him as soon as Searle's body blocked the view. He didn't wait. He grabbed Searle's legs and twisted them and felt Searle falling. He fell with him, to the landing, which was another half dozen steps below. He began flailing away at Searle's head and shoulders. He heard shouts of "Fight! Fight!" He heard his name being yelled. "Beekman's beating up Searle." He felt hands pulling at him, trying to separate him from Searle, who was crying out for help. He heard Marcus imploring him to give it up. He felt Marcus tugging at him. He felt the heavy hands of an adult yank him to his feet. It was Mr. Keen.

"He started it," Searle yelled. "He pushed me down the stairs."

Beekman looked at Searle, whose nose was bleeding. He looked at Mr. Keen and saw how angry he was. He ran the rest of the way down the stairs and out the door to the street.

# 23

## On the Run

Beekman ran like the wind. His arms and legs pumped like firing pistons. He ran into Central Park, then headed south along its western edge, past the lake and Strawberry Fields to the Sheep Meadow. He imagined himself a wild horse running across the plains. Nothing could stop him. He cut across the Sheep Meadow and headed east until he came to the zoo. His lungs burned. His foot throbbed. His ribs ached as his breath shot out in front of him in short frosty bursts. He sat on a bench to rest.

He'd made a mistake fighting Searle. He'd lost control. It looked like he'd started it. Mr. Keen had caught him on top of Searle, bloodying his nose. Tomorrow he'd be called into the mighty McCann's office and expelled. Leo would be disappointed, then he would find him a new school and they wouldn't be able to pay for that one either. What difference did it make why he had to leave? He told himself it didn't matter.

All that remained was Mary Louise. If he hurried to Wembley Hall he could be there when she came out. He'd make it count for something.

He started walking, favoring his bad leg, feeling the pain from all those punches to his body. With each step he picked up his pace. He started running, slowly at first, then faster. Until he was flying.

She came out in the company of the same two friends who had walked her to the dance. There was no time to catch his breath. She started up the street.

"Mary Louise!" Beekman shouted.

She kept going.

"Emily Elizabeth Dickinson was born in 1830," he shouted.

Mary Louise stopped and looked back.

"In Amherst, Massachusetts," Beekman shouted. "She had a brother and a sister. She was mostly a recluse. Her poems are filled with feeling and original thinking."

He saw her staring at him. He was quite sure he saw her smile.

"She understood love and other emotions," he shouted. "She was intense and sensitive. Like somebody else I know. After she died in 1886, her sister found over a thousand of her poems hidden in a bureau. I know a lot about Emily Dickinson."

Mary Louise looked at Beekman for what seemed an eternity, then walked off.

"I read a book about her," he shouted. "I thought it was something we could talk about."

Mary Louise turned the corner.

Beekman jammed his hands into his pockets and limped off, hurting, convinced that his life was crashing down around him the way a building collapses on itself when it is imploded with dynamite.

# 24

## The Way Out

"It was the crowd of boys at the top of the stairs that drew me to it," Mr. Keen said, responding to a question from the mighty McCann.

"And what did you see when you got there?" the mighty McCann asked.

"I saw Beekman—Mr. O'Day—hitting Mr. Searle."

"Did you at any time see Mr. Searle hitting Mr. O'Day?"

"No," Mr. Keen said, "but I've thought about it and I don't believe for a minute that Beekman wasn't somehow driven to it. He's not the sort of boy who would hit somebody without cause."

"He hit me," Searle said, sticking his face out into the light where the mighty McCann could get a better view of exhibit A. Searle's left eye was swollen. The welts on his face looked like little ripe plums. "He hit me and I didn't do anything to make him."

"I'll get to you in a minute," the mighty McCann said. He turned back to Mr. Keen. "Did you see anything to indicate that Mr. O'Day was defending himself?"

Mr. Keen searched his memory. He looked at Beekman, then at Searle, then at Beekman's father, then at Marcus, then at the mighty McCann again. Beekman could tell that Mr. Keen was trying to help him. He knew it was impossible.

"I didn't see anything specific," Mr. Keen said finally, "but I know what I know. Beekman didn't start it."

The mighty McCann nodded and turned to Searle. "We'll hear your side of it now."

"Beekman snuck up behind me," Searle said, "then pushed me down the stairs. Then he hit me. That's what happened."

"He just pushed you?" the mighty McCann asked. "For no reason at all?"

"I was coming to see you," Searle said. "That's why. He was bothering me all day just because I called him

Beek the geek. He was punching me and grabbing me and it was making me crazy. He wouldn't stop. I told him I was going to tell you. He was afraid you were going to kick him out of school. So he pushed me and jumped on top of me and hit me."

The mighty McCann considered all this. "I see," he said at last, as though he didn't see at all. "It's your story that Mr. O'Day, who is half your size, spent the day attacking you, and that you didn't respond in any way, and that he pushed you down the stairs and hit you when you said you were coming to see me?"

"That's it," Searle said. "That's exactly what he said. Are you going to throw him out now?"

"You can leave, Mr. Searle," the mighty McCann said. "Thank you for your trouble, Mr. Keen."

"Don't believe a word of it," Mr. Keen said to the mighty McCann. "I'd bet anything on Beekman's innocence."

"Thank you, Mr. Keen," the mighty McCann said again.

"He's guilty," Searle said.

Mr. Keen took Searle by the arm and guided him from the office. The mighty McCann turned his attention to Marcus.

"Mr. Peavy, I understand you have something to add to all this," the mighty McCann said.

Marcus stood like a lawyer about to address the court. He cleared his throat. He approached the mighty McCann until he was standing directly in front of his desk.

"Beekman is my best friend," Marcus said. "I feel it's my duty to inform you of that before I begin."

"Yes, yes," the mighty McCann said impatiently. "Let's get on with it."

"I was aware all day yesterday," Marcus said, "that Searle was doing something to Beekman. He was outside every class waiting for us. He sat next to Beekman at lunch, which he never does."

"Did you see Mr. Searle hit Mr. O'Day?" the mighty McCann asked. "Did you see Mr. Searle do anything to Mr. O'Day?"

"I saw Searle holding on to Beekman like he was keeping him from getting away," Marcus said. "I saw Searle talking to Beekman like he was threatening him. I didn't see Searle hit Beekman, but I'm certain he did. It's the only explanation that makes sense."

"Did Mr. O'Day say anything to you about Mr. Searle? Did Mr. O'Day complain about Mr. Searle's behavior?"

"I asked Beekman what was going on, but he wouldn't tell me."

"Anything else?"

"Yes," Marcus said. "Beekman didn't do it."

"He didn't hit Mr. Searle?"

"Oh, he hit him all right," Marcus said. "He just didn't start it."

Marcus left. It was Beekman's turn. He looked at his father, who was sitting on the couch looking back at him intently. Leo hadn't said a word since the call from Miss Haymaker requesting his presence at this meeting. Beekman had already told him about the fight by then. He'd already accepted the blame. As long as he had to leave Chance, he might as well get it over with.

"What do you have to say for yourself?" the mighty McCann asked Beekman.

"I have nothing to say," Beekman said.

"Nothing at all?"

"There isn't anything to say," Beekman said.

"Why would Beekman attack somebody twice his size if he didn't have a good reason?" Leo asked. "This kid Searle has been bothering my son since the day he started here. You heard what Marcus Peavy said. You heard Mr. Keen."

"I know how you must feel," the mighty McCann

said to Leo. "I'd defend my son too. Unfortunately, he's on probation. He knew what would happen to him the next time he found himself in trouble."

The mighty McCann turned slowly to Beekman. "It gives me no pleasure to say it," he said. "You're expelled."

# 25

## Beekman's Fortune

"Why did you fight that boy?" Leo asked Beekman. They were standing on the sidewalk in front of Chance Academy.

"There was no other way," Beekman said.

"I don't accept that," Leo said. "If this Searle started it, you should have said so. If you started it, you should have owned up to it. You should have told Headmaster McCann why you started it. Why didn't you say anything? Why didn't you defend yourself?"

"I'm sorry I let you down," Beekman said.

"You let yourself down," Leo said. "That's the main thing."

They ate dinner quickly and in silence. Beekman

found no comfort in his bed. When he fell asleep finally, he had a dream about falling. In the morning Leo made them pancakes. There were a half dozen cases of pancake mix stacked on the kitchen floor.

"I want to know what that kid Searle did to you," Leo said.

"What difference does it make?" Beekman responded.

"I know he did something," Leo said. "I know you didn't start it. What happened?"

"I got thrown out of school," Beekman said. "It's happened before. It'll probably happen again."

"That's it?" Leo said. "That's all you've got to say?"

"You could send me to public school," Beekman said.

"I'm not going to let you fall through the cracks, because there are too many kids in your class and not enough teachers to help you when you need it. I'm going to get you educated whether you like it or not. I'm not going to give up on you."

Leo pushed himself away from the counter, leaving most of his breakfast uneaten. "I have to go," he said. "I have a busy day."

"Don't worry about me," Beekman said.

"But I do worry about you, son of mine," Leo said. "I worry about you all the time. I want you to stay here and spend the day thinking about this. You have to grow up. You have to start taking responsibility for yourself."

Leo put on his coat and opened the door. "I'll find you another school," he said as he closed it.

When his father was gone, Beekman realized that they hadn't stood in front of the mirror together. They hadn't sung a song and danced a dance. His father hadn't told him to have a great day because they were all great. Well, they weren't all great and he wasn't going to allow himself to care about the morning ritual or Chance Academy or Nutting Court or anything else. He washed the breakfast dishes and put them away.

He went to his room. He eyed the book on Emily Dickinson. He'd get Marcus to take it back. He wondered if he'd ever see Marcus again. He wondered if Mary Louise would ever talk to him. That part of his life was most likely over too. He wasn't going to let himself miss either one of them. He got dressed. He could barely get his shoe over his swollen foot. He couldn't tie the laces.

He went back downstairs. He looked out the window. It was beginning to rain. He looked at the clock. Barely twenty minutes had passed since his father's departure. He wondered why time moved so quickly when he was happy and so slowly when he wasn't.

He found himself thinking about the time he'd gotten his head stuck between two pillars of the small balcony outside the apartment on Seventy-fourth Street where he and Leo had lived when he was four. The fire department had to come. They'd chipped away at the pillars and greased his head and finally pried him loose. Leo hadn't been mad at him then either. Just plenty aggravated.

He looked at the clock again. Another ten minutes had evaporated. The rain was coming down harder. In a better world, a fairer one, he'd be in English class. He cast his gaze in the direction of Madam de Campo's house.

"Everything is exactly ready," she said when she opened the door to let him in.

Two chairs faced each other across the round table in the center of the room. At the table's center, exposed now, was a flawless crystal ball. It was filled with a purple haze.

"Let me see your hands," Madam de Campo said. "Wash them," she said after her inspection. "Sit down," she said when he returned from the bathroom. "Put your hands on top of the crystal ball," she said.

Beekman stretched his arms as far as they would go. "They won't reach," he said.

"Then you'll have to stand," she said.

He stood and placed his hands on the crystal ball. Madam de Campo put her hands on top of his. They were warm, like she'd just taken them from the oven.

"Look at me," she said. "Look at my eyes and keep looking at them. Don't look at anything else."

Beekman felt the ball begin to vibrate gently beneath his hands. He glanced at it and saw that the whole thing had turned purple.

"Don't look away," Madam de Campo said. "If you look away, I won't be able to see anything."

He fixed his eyes on hers, wondering how long he could hold them that way, and a moment later forgot where he was and what he was doing.

"Turmoil," Madam de Campo said. "Trouble. Anger. Guilt. Doubt. Unhappiness. You think you're alone in the world, but you're not. We're all connected. We need each other. Never forget that."

The vibrations from the ball worked their way up Beekman's arms and invaded his head. He heard the music of a tuning fork.

"Everything changes," Madam de Campo said. "Nothing stays the same. Some of your dreams will come true. Hold on to the rest of them. Dreams require faith. Faith requires life. Life requires risks."

"What's that mean?" Beekman asked. It sounded to him like his voice was coming from another room. "What's going to happen to me?"

"Most of what you want, you'll get," she said.

"Hooey," Beekman said.

"Hooey? What's hooey?"

"What you're saying is hooey," Beekman said. "It doesn't mean anything."

"Life isn't hooey," Madam de Campo said.

"Is my father going to marry Fernanda?" Beekman asked.

"Who knows?" Madam de Campo said.

"Are we going to stay at Nutting Court?"

"Will this happen? Will that happen? All I can say is that sooner or later, school, friendships, life in general, most of it will make you happy."

"Hooey!" Beekman shouted.

"There you go with that word again."

"You don't know anything," Beekman said, pulling his hands free. "You didn't tell me anything." He headed for the door. "My life is not working out. I got expelled from school. I don't have any friends. Nothing changes. Ever."

"What about the big deal?" Madam de Campo asked.

"What big deal?" Beekman stopped by the door.

"Something's in the works," she said.

"Is my father going to make a big deal?" Beekman asked. "Is that what you're saying?"

"I don't know whose deal it is," she said. "All I know is that it's big."

"You don't know anything," Beekman said for the second time. He marched out and returned, limping through the rain, to his house.

Waiting for the rest of the day to pass was like watching concrete dry. Each second that ticked by seemed to take an eternity, and with the passing of each second, Beekman's body protested more and more the treatment it had received at Searle's hands. He could feel each fist and elbow. His foot was so badly swollen, he had to remove his shoe. Finally, all he could think of to do was to sink his body into a tub of hot water. It was the closest thing to the steam bath he sometimes took with his father after working out. He'd always felt better afterwards.

He filled the tub and slowly lowered himself into it, until his body was completely submerged. Only his face broke the surface, a small island of mouth, nose, and eyes in the middle of the ocean. He felt the pain easing. He closed his eyes. He felt like he was floating on currents of warm, sweet air. The door flew open.

"Sorry to barge in on you," Leo said, heading for the toilet. "Emergency pee."

Beekman sat straight up he was so startled. "What are you doing home so early?"

Leo flushed. "Did you think about what happened at school yesterday?" he asked. "Are you ready to talk about it?" Leo washed his hands.

"Why do we have to talk about it?" Beekman asked. "Why can't we just forget about it?"

"Because I don't want it to happen again," Leo said. He looked over at Beekman. "What's that on your shoulders?"

"Nothing," Beekman said, slipping back under the water as fast as he could.

Leo moved to the edge of the tub and looked down at the marks all over his son's body.

# 26

## Restoration

His father had him by the tight grip of a hand as he hopped, jumped, limped, and otherwise slid across the highly polished marble floor of Chance Academy's grand entry. They charged right past Miss Haymaker.

"I'm going to have a word with the headmaster," Leo said without slowing down.

"Go right in," Miss Haymaker said, making it sound like this was something that happened every morning at three minutes before nine.

The mighty McCann was putting on his black chapel robe when Leo barged in, Beekman in tow.

"This won't take long," Leo said to the mighty Mc-Cann. "Take off your shirt," he told Beekman.

"What do you want here?" the mighty McCann asked. He wasn't pleased. "This has all been settled."

"Not yet it hasn't," Leo said.

Beekman unbuttoned the last of his shirt buttons.

"I won't be late for chapel," the mighty McCann said, moving out of his office and into Miss Haymaker's. "We'll do this another time. Make an appointment."

Leo followed the headmaster. "Get out here," he said to Beekman. He put a hand on the mighty McCann's arm to stop him.

"Look at my son," Leo said. "Look what that boy did to him."

Beekman moved into Miss Haymaker's office in his undershirt.

"Take it off," Leo said.

Beekman pulled his undershirt over his head. He heard Miss Haymaker gasp. The mighty McCann moved closer. He examined the bruises that were spread over Beekman's chest and back and sides.

"Mr. Searle did this to you?" the mighty McCann asked.

"He did," Beekman said.

"Why didn't you say so yesterday? Why did you make us go through all that? Put your shirt on and come to chapel. We'll sort this out later." The mighty McCann nodded at Leo and roared off.

Beekman buttoned his shirt and stuffed it into his pants as quickly as he could. "You got me back in," he said to his father, "but I'll just have to leave again when you can't pay the bill."

"Who can't pay the bill?" Leo said. "Of course I can pay it. I've got a big one about to break."

"There aren't any big ones," Beekman said.

"What are you talking about?" Leo said. "Where'd you hear that? There are big ones everywhere. All over the place. Just around the corner. Business is picking up. That Alaska deal looks better every hour."

Beekman wanted to believe his father, but how was that possible after what he'd discovered? He wanted to yell out that he knew everything. But that would hurt Leo and, as angry as Beekman was, he wanted that least of all.

"I didn't mean to cause all this trouble," Beekman said.

"Next time speak up for yourself," Leo said.

Beekman hopped off after the mighty McCann, who was waiting for him by the chapel door. "Hurry along, Mr. O'Day," the mighty McCann urged. "A young man in your position can't afford to be late."

At noon, Beekman was called back to the mighty McCann's office. Marcus was there, along with Wibble and Foyle.

"Mr. Peavy has done a bit of detective work," the mighty McCann said. "He's persuaded these gentlemen to step forward. It seems that Mr. Wibble saw Mr. Searle hitting you on a number of occasions. He was afraid to speak up for fear of becoming the next victim. Is that correct, Mr. Wibble?"

"I saw him doing it all day," Wibble said.

"Mr. Foyle, it seems, saw Mr. Searle push you down the stairs," the mighty McCann said. "His reluctance to say anything stemmed from the same fear. Is that correct, Mr. Foyle?"

"Yes, sir," Foyle said.

"In addition to which," the mighty McCann said, "Miss Haymaker informs me that Mr. Searle created a disturbance at the Wembley Hall dance. Accordingly, I have expelled Mr. Searle and reinstated you. The incident is now closed. You have work to do, Mr. O'Day. I suggest you get cracking." The mighty McCann dismissed them with a wave of his hand.

"That turned out well," Marcus said as he and Beekman climbed the stairs to the second floor.

Beekman didn't think so at all. The longer he stayed at Chance, the harder it would be to leave.

"Thanks," Beekman said. There was no point in making Marcus feel bad. He'd helped him after all.

"You'd do the same for me," Marcus said.

He looked at Marcus, who was loud and right in your face a lot of the time, who was awkward and goofy all the time, and realized that it was true. Marcus Peavy was the last person in the world he'd expected to have for a friend.

That afternoon, Mr. Nussbaum hit Beekman on the head with a blackboard eraser. "You missed class yesterday, Mr. O'Day," Mr. Nussbaum said. Chalk dust exploded into the air. "You've got some serious catching up to do."

workouts with Leo were paying off. He'd been accepted, at long last, by his classmates. He was simply one of them now, no more, no less.

Thanksgiving dinner at Nutting Court was hosted by Minnie and Manfried Mumm. It was their turn. There was turkey, stuffing, cranberry sauce, mashed potatoes, sweet potatoes, peas, those little onions that look like pearls, and Brussels sprouts. Enough to sink a ship.

Afterwards, groaning and moaning from the overload, the residents of Nutting Court headed out for a walk. By Thirty-fourth Street they'd spread out. Moxie, Loomis, and Sergio led the way. They were followed by Edna, Larry, Minnie, and Manfried. Leo and Fernanda were next. They held hands, a most positive sign in Beekman's estimation. He ended up with Madam de Campo, which suited him fine.

"I shouldn't have said it was hooey," Beekman said.

"I've grown quite fond of that word," Madam de Campo said.

"It wasn't hooey," Beekman said. "You were right."

"Then things are good?"

"Things are excellent," Beekman said.

Madam de Campo placed a purple gloved hand on Beekman's shoulder and gave it a squeeze. "The

# 27

## Giving Thanks

By Thanksgiving, Beekman had come to see things in a new light. He'd decided that Madam de Campo had been right all along. Because, first of all, somewhere, somehow, Leo had gotten his hands on the money to pay the Chance Academy bill. Enough of it anyway to keep him in school. For that he was thankful. He was, in fact, with the exception of his difficulties with Mary Louise Peavy, thankful for many things.

He'd started to flourish at Chance. He worked hard and arrived on time and performed progressively better on his tests and, on rare occasion, caught the mighty McCann eyeing him with approval. Even Mr. Jack was beginning to show him some respect. The courage of your convictions," she said. "That's what counts."

Hot apple pie with a slice of cheese or a scoop of vanilla ice cream was served upon their return.

The next day, Beekman and Leo and Fernanda went to the movies, then to Mr. Chin's for dinner. It was the first time he'd been included in their plans. He spent a lot of the weekend alone. Leo and Fernanda were busy and Marcus and Mary Louise had gone off to spend the holiday with Grandmother Peavy in Connecticut. Beekman slogged through his homework like a ditch digger, then turned to the great unfinished business of his life. To that end, he spent Sunday afternoon with Moxie LaMoca. Then it was Monday and back to school.

At the corner where they parted company, Leo gave his son an extra long look. "I have a feeling this is going to be an outstanding day," Leo said.

"So do I," Beekman said. "Today is Operation Mary Louise Peavy."

"She's a lucky young woman," Leo said. "Me, I'm working on the single biggest deal of my life. A rich Brazilian wants to start an airline and I may have found him a dozen old jets. I'll know today. It's the one we've been waiting for, son of mine."

"Knock 'em dead, Pop," Beekman said.

"Good luck with Operation Mary Louise Peavy," Leo said. He gave his son a playful poke in the shoulder.

Beekman gave him one back, then headed for the bus stop. Today was the day he'd strike at the heart of the matter. He'd need all the good luck he could get.

# 28

## Emily Lives

"This is stupid," Marcus said.

"It's not stupid."

"It is."

"It's failure-proof," Beekman said.

"It's stupid."

"It's dramatic."

"It's stupid."

"Will you stop saying it's stupid," Beekman said. "It's brilliant. Quit complaining. You said you'd help me." That Marcus couldn't see the beauty of his plan was annoying. "A little support wouldn't hurt."

"I'm here, aren't I?" Marcus said. "I don't want to be, but I am. If you're so far gone that you think my sister is attractive in some way, then what choice do I have but to be here? Somebody has to pick up the pieces. But it's still stupid."

"It is not stupid," Beekman said.

The high-arched double doors opened and the first of Wembley Hall's young ladies moved through them to the sidewalk. Beekman watched and waited. Marcus stood at his side, his expression filled with Mount Rushmore–sized skepticism.

"Get ready," Beekman said. He'd gone over the routine a dozen times with Moxie, but he was still anxious. He shivered in the cold.

"I'm ready," Marcus said. "This is stupid," he added under his breath.

Beekman started to tell Marcus that he had Madam de Campo's fortune on his side. That this was his destiny. But just then he saw Mary Louise make her way from the building. Her face was puffy and her eyes were red. She sneezed. She blew her nose. She looked miserable. He was about to change all that.

"Let me have it," Beekman said.

"Here," Marcus said, slapping it into Beekman's hand.

Beekman pulled the wig down on his head and tore off his coat and raced across the street in the long Victorian dress that Moxie had made for him.

"Mary Louise!" Beekman called out. "Mary Louise!"

She turned and her mouth opened, but nothing came out. She was speechless.

"I'm Emily Dickinson," Beekman rasped.

She laughed, but she didn't look happy.

"I've come all the way from Amherst to recite one of my poems."

Mary Louise ran.

" 'To make a prairie it takes a clover and one bee,' " Beekman shouted, running after her, which wasn't easy because of the dress.

" 'One clover, and a bee,' " he shouted, " 'And revery.' "

The distance between them was growing. She was fast.

" 'The revery alone will do / If bees are few,' " he shouted. There. He'd done it. He'd gotten it right.

He hiked up his dress and ran as hard as he could.

"I was hoping you'd show me your poems," he shouted. "Then we could discuss them."

Mary Louise reached the corner and was gone.

"It's a long trip from Massachusetts," Beekman shouted. "You could at least thank me for coming."

His heart pounding with despair, he turned back and saw that practically the entire student body of Wembley Hall had gathered to watch his performance.

"What are you looking at?" Beekman croaked at them. "Haven't you ever seen anybody in a dress before?"

The young ladies of Wembley Hall applauded and cheered. Beekman ran to Marcus.

"I told you it was stupid," Marcus said.

"Not as stupid as what I'm going to do next," Beekman said, putting on his coat and charging off.

"Where are we going?" Marcus asked.

"Your place," Beekman said.

When they got there, Beekman went straight to Mary Louise's room.

"Go away," she said from behind her closed door when he knocked.

"No," Beekman said. "I'm not going away. Not until you talk to me and find out that I'm not a big drip like you think I am, even if I am friends with your brother."

"Go away," she said.

"You can't spend the rest of your life in your room," Beekman said. "You have to come out and be with people and do things."

"Go away."

"You're not the easiest person in the world, you know," he said. "And you're not the best-looking either. And there are actually some people who are

**192**

smarter than you. There's always somebody who's more of something. But I think you're perfect. So stop being mad at me."

"Go away," Mary Louise said.

Beekman changed his clothes and said goodbye to Elizabeth, who gave him a large brownie for the trip home. He thanked Marcus for helping him and left.

# 29

## The Bomb

"How'd it go with Operation Mary Louise Peavy?" Leo asked when Beekman walked in.

"It was a disaster," Beekman said. "I made a spectacle of myself. All she ever says to me is 'Go away.'"

"Maybe she doesn't like you," Leo said.

"How would she know?" Beekman asked. "One conversation. That's all I'm asking. If she tells me to go away after that, I'm gone." He didn't even want to contemplate the possibility.

"Give her time and try again," Leo said. "But don't be a pain about it. Come sit down over here." Leo was on the couch, a glass of beer and a pad of yellow legal paper in front of him. His tie was loosened, his sleeves rolled up. He looked tired. "We'll have ourselves a conversation, then go out for dinner."

"I thought you were having dinner with Fernanda."

"I called it off."

"Why?"

"We're in the middle of a slight disagreement right now."

"You had a fight?" The alarm bells went off.

"It's nothing to get upset about."

But he was upset. More than upset. His father and Fernanda were supposed to be a matter of clear sailing. "Did you fight about me?" he asked. Leo came with a twelve-year-old son. A twelve-year-old son could get in the way.

"It had nothing to do with you," Leo said. "It was about me and the future. About me not having much of one. About it being pointless for her to spend any more time with me. Sit down here."

"You're going to make up with her, aren't you?" Beekman asked. He sat next to his father.

"We have to talk about the future too, son of mine," Leo said. "The airplane deal didn't work out. Nothing has worked out in quite a while. Not even the little deals."

"There are no little deals," Beekman said. He was trying not to show how worried he was.

"It's been a long dry spell," Leo said.

"Things will get better," Beekman said. He'd have to think of something to bring his father and Fernanda back together. Quickly.

"Of course things will get better," Leo said. "Things always get better. Meanwhile, we have to find ourselves a new situation."

"No!" Beekman jumped to his feet and banged his knee into the coffee table. "No more new situations. I'm not moving. That's it!" His knee felt like it was going to burst into flames.

"You're old enough to have it straight," Leo said. "We had three months to come up with the down payment for this place."

"You said if we liked it we could stay."

"The three months are up."

"Well, I like it and I'm staying," Beekman said. His knee hurt so bad he wanted to scream.

"I like it here too," Leo said, "but I don't have the money and that's the arrangement I made with the lawyer who represents the owner. We buy or we move."

"We had a deal," Beekman said, his voice growing raspier and raspier. "You promised. We shook on it."

"I thought it would work out," Leo said. "It didn't. The money didn't come in. Not for this place. Probably not for your January tuition at Chance. I might be able to come up with that, but I wouldn't count on anything. There's nothing I can do."

"There's something I can do," Beekman said.

"We're moving," Leo said. "We're shifting into tight times in the O'Day family."

Beekman headed for the stairs. "I'm not leaving here," he said.

"We don't have any choice," Leo said. "We have to be out over the weekend."

"You can be out over the weekend," Beekman shouted. He grabbed his backpack and ran up the stairs. "I'm staying."

Beekman slammed the door behind him and locked it. He propped the back of his chair under the doorknob.

"I'm not going anywhere," he shouted at the top of his lungs.

# 30

## Beekman's Big Deal

Beekman heard his father climbing the stairs. "You can't come in here," he shouted. "You're not invited. The door is locked."

"Come on, Beekman," Leo pleaded. "This isn't going to get us anywhere."

"Why did you even bother to get me back into school?" Beekman rasped. "Why did you tell me things were getting better?"

"They were," Leo said. "I thought they were. Deals don't always work out. You know that."

"Tell the owner we want a new deal," Beekman said. "Get more time."

"I don't know who the owner is," Leo said. "And I already asked the lawyer and he said no."

"I'm tired of moving," Beekman said.

"So am I," Leo said.

"I like it here," Beekman said.

"So do I," Leo said.

"I don't want to leave."

"I wish that's how it was," Leo said. "I wish none of this was happening. Look, I'll make a deal with you . . ."

"No!" Beekman shouted, cutting Leo off. "I'll make a deal with you." He was standing just inside the door, ready to push against it if his father tried to get in. "Number one," Beekman said, "we're not moving. This is where we're going to live from now on. Nutting Court is it."

"Please, will you let me in so we can talk," Leo implored. "All you're doing is making it more difficult."

"Number two," Beekman said, "I'm staying at Chance. I'll get a job. I'll do anything. I don't care how hard it is. Number three, you and Fernanda will make up and then you'll get married. Number four, you'll get a regular job. Something that pays money every week. Do we have a deal?"

The telephone started to ring downstairs.

"Do we have a deal?" Beekman shouted.

"I have to answer the phone," Leo said. "I'll be right back."

"Do we have a deal?" Beekman shouted again. He didn't think he was asking too much. He didn't think it was more than was possible.

"That was a lead on an apartment in the Village," Leo yelled from the bottom of the stairs. "I have to check it out right now or it will be gone. What do you say we look at it together?"

"I'm not going to look at anything," Beekman yelled back. "I already have a place to live."

"I'll see you in a little while then," Leo yelled. "I understand why you're mad at me, but it's not going to change anything."

"I'm staying here forever," Beekman yelled.

A minute later Beekman heard his father leave. He watched through his window as Leo stopped to look at Fernanda's house, then walked off, his stride as relaxed and confident as ever.

Beekman pulled the chair away, unlocked the door, and hurried down the stairs to the bathroom. Then he gathered supplies: a half-filled jar of crunchy peanut butter, a box of wheat crackers, two small apples, a knife to spread the peanut butter, the last three chocolate chip cookies, the last bottle of water, a roll of toilet paper, and the bucket they used for cleaning.

When he was back in his room and his supplies were stowed, he looked through his mother's things. He went through them slowly. He was certain she'd approve of what he was doing.

"It was already taken," Leo said upon his return. He climbed the stairs slowly. "I stopped and got us a pizza. Half pepperoni, half plain."

Leo sat on the floor outside Beekman's door and removed a slice of pepperoni from the box and started eating. "I'd slide a slice under the door," he said, "but it won't fit."

"I'm not hungry," Beekman said. The aroma of cooked tomatoes and melted mozzarella and warm, chewy crust filled his nostrils. He could taste it.

"Open the door and I'll pass you a slice," Leo said. "I'll eat mine out here and you eat yours in there and we'll talk."

"I'm not coming out," Beekman said.

"I have a couple of leads to check out in the morning," Leo said. "We'll have a new place tomorrow."

"You'll have a new place," Beekman said.

Leo gathered up the pizza box and headed downstairs. "Good night, son of mine," he said. "Sleep tight."

"I'm not going to sleep," Beekman yelled. "I'm going to stand guard. I'm going to stay up all night. I'm going to stay in here until I'm an old man. Someday all you'll find is a pile of bones."

Beekman unscrewed the top off the jar of peanut butter. He spread some on a chocolate chip cookie.

# 31

## The Board of Directors

"Up and at 'em," Leo shouted. He banged on Beekman's door.

"I am up and at 'em," Beekman said. His father's voice had startled him to wakefulness. He didn't remember falling asleep. "Rudy used to say that," he said, rubbing his eyes. "Remember Rudy?"

"Who could forget Rudy?" Leo said. "Get a move on, my boy. School is at hand."

"I'm not going to school," Beekman said.

"You'll be expelled if you miss another day," Leo said.

"So what?" Beekman said. "I'm out of there anyway."

"If you get expelled, it won't make any difference if I can afford it," Leo said. "You'll be gone."

"He won't expel me when he finds out why I'm not there."

"I'm coming in," Leo said. "I've had enough of this." Leo's voice carried an edge that Beekman had heard only a few times in his life. "I'll break the door down if I have to."

"I'll barricade myself in the storage area," Beekman said.

"I'll break that door down too."

"You can't break down any doors," Beekman said. "You can't come in here. If you do, you'll be breaking another deal. The only one we have left."

Leo pounded on the door. "Beekman! Open the door! Now!"

"Do we have a deal?" Beekman yelled. He was standing by his closet, ready to dive into the storage area and block its entrance with boxes.

Leo took a deep breath. "I'm going to look for apartments," he said. "When I get back I expect you to be at school. When you get home, we'll start packing."

But Beekman couldn't go to school, because if he did it would mean he'd accepted what was happening. He'd have given up without a fight. There'd be no hope after that. Nothing would change.

He watched his father leave. A few minutes later he saw Madam de Campo emerge from her house, wrapped in her purple cape, her purple scarf wrapped around her neck, her purple hat pulled down over her ears. He pulled the chair away from the door, unlocked it, and ran down the stairs.

"It was all hooey," Beekman yelled at Madam de Campo as he flung open the door and ran into the alley. "Everything you said was hooey. We have to move now. We can't buy this house the way we were supposed to. I can't stay in school. Nothing worked out. There was no big deal. You were wrong. You shouldn't tell people things are going to happen if they're not."

"That's a lot of bad news," Madam de Campo said. "I had no idea."

"You were supposed to have an idea," Beekman said. "You were supposed to know. This is where I want to be. This is where I'm staying."

He ran inside and slammed the door behind him and raced up the stairs and slammed his bedroom door and locked it and jammed the back of the chair up under the doorknob and cried. About his mother and school and moving. About what was happening between him and his father. About how nothing ever lasted. It came bursting out. He used up half a roll of toilet paper blowing his nose. When he was done he fell into a deep sleep. He dreamed that he was lost and that no one would help him. Then he heard his name being called. The voice grew louder.

"Beekman," the voice called. "Beekman. Beekman."

He jumped from the bed and caught his foot in the covers and fell to the floor and landed on the knee that he'd knocked into the coffee table the night before.

"Ow!" he yelled. He grabbed his knee. He gritted his teeth.

"Beekman," the voice called, "are you all right in there?" It was Madam de Campo.

"Go away," Beekman said, thinking he was beginning to sound a lot like Mary Louise Peavy. His knee throbbed.

"Open the door," Madam de Campo said.

"No," Beekman said.

"We have business to discuss," Madam de Campo said.

"Is my father out there?"

"I don't know where your father is."

"Then how did you get into my house?"

"I have a key," Madam de Campo said. "I have keys to all the houses. In case there's an emergency. Please open the door."

"Whatever you have to say you can say from out there," Beekman said.

"There are too many of us to do it that way," Madam de Campo said. "It has to be face-to-face."

"If my father's not with you, who is?" Beekman asked.

"The board of directors of Nutting Court," Madam de Campo said.

"What's that?" Beekman asked. "I never heard of it."

"We've just held a special meeting," Madam de Campo said. "We have something to tell you. When we're done, we'll leave and you can lock the door again. It'll take two minutes."

He watched them enter: Madam de Campo, then Fernanda Bloom, Moxie LaMoca, Sergio West, Edna and Larry Biggs, Loomis Garcia, and Minnie and Manfried Mumm. They stood together in a tight knot, their heads bent to avoid the ceiling. Except for Minnie and Manfried, who could pretty much look Beekman in the eye.

"Everybody who owns a house at Nutting Court is on the board of directors," Madam de Campo said. "Each house gets one vote, except that I get two when there's a tie. So I can break it. That's because I'm a Nutting. The last Nutting left. I set it up this way. You only get to live here if we all want you. For someone wanting to live here, the vote has to be unanimous."

They were all smiling at him. Beekman didn't understand why. What was Madam de Campo talking about?

"We wanted somebody young to move in," Madam de Campo continued. "We wanted some new life. Some energy. And the very day we decided that, our lawyer called about Leo O'Day and his twelve-year-old son. We decided to give you three months. To see if you were the right ones. We've decided that you are."

"But the lawyer said we had to leave," Beekman said.

"I told the lawyer to say that," Madam de Campo said. "To see how much you really wanted to live here. To see if you wanted us as much as we want you."

"We've watched you from the beginning," Moxie said.

"And we've liked what we've seen," Minnie said.

"You're who we want," Loomis said.

"And since that's so," Fernanda said, "we've voted to sell you this house and let you pay for it when you can."

"We have the money in the Nutting Court Trust to do it that way," Madam de Campo said.

"It's how we operate," Sergio said.

"It's how we bought our house," Edna said.

"My great-great-grandfather built Nutting Court for his family," Madam de Campo said. "Now it's a different kind of family and we want you to be part of it."

"You mean we can stay," Beekman said.

"That's exactly what I mean," Madam de Campo said.

# 32

## All's Well That Ends Well

Leo protested when he heard Madam de Campo's offer. "I don't have the money," he said. "I may never have the money. I can't make that kind of commitment."

"Nonsense," Madam de Campo said.

For every reason Leo came up with not to do it, the board of directors of Nutting Court came up with two reasons why he should. Why he must. But Leo kept balking.

It was Beekman who settled it. "I can go back upstairs," he said, "and I can lock myself in my room, or you could say okay and we wouldn't have to go through all that. This is the place, Pop."

Leo gave his son a long, hard look. Then he smiled.

"Okay," he said. "This is the place." He turned to the board of directors of Nutting Court.

"We accept your offer," Leo said to them. "And we thank you."

There were hugs and handshakes all around.

Madam de Campo said she'd take care of the paperwork.

Fernanda suggested that she and Leo take a walk.

The next morning Beekman and his father stood in front of the mirror inspecting themselves and each other.

"You're looking good this morning, Pop," Beekman said.

"You're looking good yourself, son of mine," Leo said.

They adjusted the knots in their neckties.

"I'm glad you made up with Fernanda," Beekman said.

"We're making definite progress in that direction," Leo said.

"Good," Beekman said. He'd make sure the progress continued. "Am I going to stay at Chance?"

"You'll stay," Leo said. "I'll arrange something with Headmaster McCann. I'll tell him I kept you out of school yesterday. Just make sure he wants to keep you after this."

"Oh, he'll want to keep me, all right," Beekman said. "You don't have to worry about that. Are you going to get a regular job?"

"Don't push your luck," Leo said.

"I guess three out of four isn't bad," Beekman said. Three out of five if he counted his failure with Mary Louise.

"Not bad!" Leo said. "Three out of four is a big deal."

"It is?"

"It's huge," Leo said. "It's a life-changer."

It was a life-changer, Beekman thought. It was true all along what his father had told him. Anything was possible.

They sang a chorus of "Side by Side," and did a dance to go with it.

They stopped at the corner where they parted company.

"It's going to be a great day," Leo said.

"They're all great," Beekman said.

"One way or another," Leo said.

On the uptown bus, Beekman thought about what he knew for sure and what he had no idea about at all. He thought about what he had and what he didn't have. He concluded that he had a lot and that nobody got everything, even if they should.

At Eighty-sixth and Park, Marcus got on the bus and sat down next to him.

"Where were you yesterday?" Marcus asked.

"Taking care of business," Beekman said. "Why? You miss me?"

"Never happen," Marcus said. "I hate to do this, but I have something for you." He pulled a blue envelope from his pocket and handed it to Beekman. "It's from my sister."